THE
DEPOSITION

THE
DEPOSITION

A MIKE CONNOLLY MYSTERY

A NOVEL

JOE HILLEY

RiverOak®

Good News in Fiction

COOK COMMUNICATIONS MINISTRIES
Colorado Springs, Colorado • Paris, Ontario
KINGSWAY COMMUNICATIONS LTD
Eastbourne, England

RiverOak® is an imprint of
Cook Communications Ministries, Colorado Springs, CO 80918
Cook Communications, Paris, Ontario
Kingsway Communications, Eastbourne, England

THE DEPOSITION
© 2007 by Joseph H. Hilley

Cover Design: Two Moore Designs
Cover Photo: © iStock

First Printing, 2007
Printed in the United States of America

1 2 3 4 5 6 7 8 9 10

ISBN 978-1-58919-101-3
LCCN 2007927306

For the real Father Scott

Won't somebody come and rescue me
I am stranded, caught in the crossfire

"Crossfire"
Stevie Ray Vaughan

One

*L*ight from a window in Sprinkle's Store cast a harsh glare across the front seat of Scott Nolan's car. He squinted and reached for the visor. Before he could lower it, the light went out. Darkness cloaked the parking lot. Moments later a woman came from the building, crossed the gravel lot, and disappeared down a trail through the bushes on the far side.

Scott checked his watch, then lowered the windows and switched off the engine. Heavy night air hung around him like a thick, wet blanket. Sweat formed along his arms. The sleeves of his shirt stuck to his skin. He loosened the cuffs and rolled them up his forearms, then unbuttoned the collar of his shirt.

Behind him he heard the whine of tires on the pavement. A truck passed pulling a boat on a trailer. After it came a motorcycle. When they were gone, the night grew quiet and still.

Before long, headlights appeared in the distance. As they came nearer, he could see that it was a car. The car slowed and turned from the pavement. Gravel crunched beneath the tires as it rolled behind him to the opposite side of the store. Scott heard the engine stop. A car door opened, then clicked closed.

Footsteps approached, coming up behind him. He glanced in the mirror but saw only the gray outline of the bushes against the evening sky. Then the passenger door opened. Scott jumped at the sound. Mike Connolly slid in beside him on the front seat.

At fifty-something, Connolly's dark hair was beginning to turn gray. He was slim and athletic, but years of drinking and hard living had left lines around the corners of his eyes and robbed his skin of its natural luster. Still, he was the best lawyer Scott knew and the only one he trusted.

Connolly glanced over at him. "What is it we have to meet out here about?"

Scott reached over the back of the seat for his jacket. He took a paper from the inside pocket and handed it to Connolly.

"They served me with this today."

Connolly looked at the document.

"It's a subpoena for a deposition."

"I know. Why do they want to talk to me?"

Connolly laid the subpoena in his lap and leaned against the car door.

"Camille Braxton's mother is suing the bank and Buie Hayford about the way they managed that trust."

Scott was puzzled.

"What trust?"

"Tonsmeyer Trust. The one I told you about. Owned that building where they had Panama Tan." Connolly grinned. "You remember Panama Tan, don't you?"

Scott ignored the needling question.

"They needed to be sued. Why do they want me?"

Connolly sighed.

"It's not you they want." He looked over at Scott. "It's me."

"You?"

"Larry King called me the other day. He wants me to testify about what happened with the tanning salon. The women. The warehouse where they had them staying. How Defuniak was in there. In the building where they were keeping them. Knew all about it."

Scott felt frustrated.

"So they depose everyone who ever knew you?"

Connolly shrugged.

"Who knows? Buie's lawyer would depose me, but he knows I'm not talking about anything. Most of what I know is privileged, and getting past that is more than he wants to get into. And even if he did, none of it would help his client." He handed the paper back to Scott. "So they're asking you about it."

"But I wasn't there. All I did was drive them over to Florida after you got them out."

A smile spread across Connolly's face.

"And you went to the tanning salon."

Scott felt his cheeks flush with the memory. He turned away. "Don't remind me."

He could feel Connolly staring at him.

"You closed your eyes. Right?"

Memories of that night swept through Scott's mind like a storm. He'd been there all right. And he'd closed his eyes—most of the time.

Scott cleared his throat.

"Any word from Raisa?"

"Not really. They say she's all right."

"Still miss her?"

"I don't know. Hey, I would have looked too."

Scott turned from the window and swung his arm toward Connolly. His hand struck Connolly on the shoulder.

"I didn't look."

Connolly laughed.

"Okay. Whatever you say."

Connolly continued to laugh.

Scott glared at him, trying to be mad, but he couldn't keep from smiling.

"Well, I might have looked a little." He slapped Connolly on the chest. "And every time you bring it up I have to work for a week to get it out of my mind."

Connolly laughed even harder. Scott leaned his head back against the seat. They both caught their breath.

"Hear from anyone else?"

"Just Victoria." Connolly chuckled. "Hollis tells me more than I want to know about her."

"How is Hollis?"

"He's fine."

"What about the others? Hear from any of them?"

"No. I think everyone else was resettled. Scattered across the country. Government couldn't really send them back. Not after all that."

Scott stared ahead out the windshield.

"Can you imagine? Someone comes to you. You think they can open the door to your dreams. Then you wake up and realize you're trapped." He looked over at Connolly. "And I mean really trapped. Economically, socially, physically."

Connolly nodded.

"And I'm sure it happens every day."

"Shuttled from place to place. Bought. Sold. Beaten. Forced to ..."

His voice trailed away.

Connolly took a breath.

"Yeah, well, we got them out." He sighed again. "And now the bank's gonna pay for it."

"Think they can win?"

"The bank?"

"No. The people who filed the lawsuit." Scott glanced at the subpoena. "Jessica Stabler."

Connolly smiled.

"Oh, yeah." He nodded. "She can win. The only real question is who goes to jail."

Scott felt the bottom drop out of his stomach. Jail. Testimony. The grand jury. There was no way Connolly could know about Tatiana. He did his best to hide the look from his face.

"Jail?"

Connolly nodded.

"A judge hears all that stuff, somebody will do some time. I mean, all the prosecutor would have to do is follow the script."

Scott felt a sense of relief.

"Yeah. I guess so."

Connolly leaned forward and opened the door.

"Anyway. We can't talk about this anymore."

Scott frowned.

"Why not?"

"Because they'll ask you if we talked. You've taken enough depositions to know that."

Scott nodded. That was a long time ago. Most days he never even thought about what he used to be.

Connolly got out of the car and pushed the door closed. He rested both hands on the door frame and leaned his head through the open window.

"Keep your eyes open. Buie's lawyer is a guy named John Somerset. He's smart and meticulous. So when you answer, make sure it's the truth, 'cause he won't forget a word you say. And watch out for Buie. He'll get as dirty as it takes to win."

Connolly stepped away. Scott started the engine and pressed a button to raise the window.

Just then Connolly leaned through the opening once more. "And whatever you do, tell the truth."

Two

---

*T*hat same evening Buie Hayford sat at his desk in his office on Spring Hill Avenue. The office was located in an old house that once had been the home of a wealthy Mobile socialite. Hayford had obtained it in a deal that turned on his intimate knowledge of the indiscretions of an influential client, using the person's missteps to his advantage in a way that gave him what he wanted and left the client grateful to him for doing it.

A big man, Hayford was gregarious and likeable. Yet beneath the smiles and backslapping lay a heart of stone. He played only for money, and he played for keeps.

Across the desk from Hayford was Perry Braxton. He'd come into Hayford's orbit when he married Camille Stabler, heir to a portion of the Tonsmeyer Family Trust and one of Hayford's wealthiest clients. Hayford had exploited Braxton's addiction to women and money as a way to gain access to the trust's assets. Braxton got the women, Hayford got rich. But Camille's untimely demise had ripped the mask off of Braxton's double life and threatened to bring down Hayford's world.

Hayford set his ginger-ale bottle on the desk.

"Sure you don't want one?"

Braxton shook his head.

"Not much for ginger ale." He grinned. "Unless you have something to put in it."

Hayford shook his head.

"Can't go back to that." He loosened his tie and unbuttoned the collar of his shirt. "That stuff will kill ya."

Both men laughed. Hayford picked up the bottle for another sip.

Braxton folded his arms across his chest.

"So you think we can find her?"

Hayford gestured with the bottle.

"Castille has a war room set up down the hall. Got his boys working night and day." He tipped his head to one side. "If that isn't enough, I know how to get more persuasive help."

"Have they found anything?"

"Got a few leads, but what we need is a picture."

"Think that priest can help?"

"I don't know." Hayford smiled. "But we're gonna find out."

Braxton leaned the chair back on its rear legs.

"You think he really went in that tanning salon?"

"I know he did. I just don't know what else he knows. That's why I suggested Somerset take his deposition."

Braxton chuckled.

"Somerset still thinks this is about the lawsuit?"

"Far as I can tell."

"Think he can win it?"

Hayford shrugged.

"I don't really care about that case. Insurance is going to cover most of it. I just don't want the FBI to get that woman in front of a grand jury. They do that, we all go to jail."

Braxton shook his head.

"Not me. I got a deal."

Hayford gave him a wry smile.

"Won't do you any good with the U.S. Attorney. They'll prosecute you under federal law. They don't care what you did with the state."

Braxton chortled.

"They can't do that. Isn't there something about 'I can't be prosecuted twice for the same crime?'"

"Yeah. But all that means is the state can't prosecute you. You dealt with the state. Got nothing to do with the federal government. I mean, not now. They get their shot too."

Braxton scowled.

"That ain't right."

Hayford smiled.

"I been practicing law a long time, and I can tell you, right or wrong, whatever the federal government wants to do, they can do."

Braxton looked away.

Hayford continued.

"You got as much in this as I do."

Braxton sighed.

"What about the tapes from the salon? Can't you get a picture of her from that?"

Hayford shook his head.

"Feds took all that." Hayford set the bottle aside and leaned forward. He rested his elbows on the desk and looked across at Braxton. "That's what I need you and J.T. to do."

Braxton frowned.

"Do what?"

"Find a picture of her." Hayford lowered his voice. "Castille found a credit card receipt from a little town over in Florida. Not too far from the house where Hollis Toombs and that priest took those women. If we had a picture, Castille could put some men on the street over there. Start asking questions."

"How are you going to get a picture of her?"

"I'm not. You are."

Braxton shifted his position in the chair.

"Me?"

"You remember what she looked like?"

Braxton grinned.

"Yeah. I remember."

Hayford frowned.

"Not that."

Braxton nodded.

"I remember what she looked like. But what's that got to do with it?"

"Use that natural creativity of yours and come up with a picture."

Just then John Glover appeared in the doorway. In his midtwenties, Glover was a student at Marshall Vocational Institute, an unaccredited school that held classes not far from Hayford's office. At night Glover attended a review seminar there, trying to retain enough law to pass the bar exam. The rest of the time he did whatever Hayford told him to do.

Hayford glanced up as Glover appeared.

"J.T. We were just talking about you."

Glover entered the room and took a seat.

"I have a class in thirty minutes. What's up?"

"I need you and Braxton to help me with this thing about the women that were working over at Panama Tan."

Glover glanced at Braxton, then back to Hayford.

"You found them?"

"Not yet." Hayford leaned back in his chair. "We need a photo of the woman."

"The one they're hiding?"

"Yeah." Hayford gave Glover a look. "Think you can find one?"

Glover shrugged.

"Maybe. Where can we look?"

Hayford's eyes darkened.

"Anywhere."

Glover thought for a minute.

"I think I know where to begin."

Hayford stood.

"Good. You and Perry work it out." He came from behind the desk and started toward the door. "I gotta go down the hall. Castille wanted to show me something."

Three

Miles away, Tatiana Perovic lay on the sofa watching television at an apartment in Gainesville, Florida. Twenty-six years old, she was tall and slender with brown hair and dark, round eyes. Those features combined with her olive complexion to create a look that made her irresistible to headhunters in her native Bosnia. They'd promised her a career in entertainment, maybe even movies. What they had given her was a life of prostitution. Shuttled from city to city, she finally landed in the United States, where she was sent to Mobile, the most unlikely place of all.

For almost a year she had been forced to sell her body to anyone with the money to pay. Working from Panama Tan, she'd been little more than a slave. Housed in a warehouse with other women like her, she was destined for a short and miserable life until that day when Scott Nolan had come to the salon.

At first all Tatiana had wanted was to get away. When the FBI approached her about cooperating with their investigation, she refused to even talk to them. Then she learned of what had been done to all those women who'd been taken away, the ones who'd worked at the salon and then disappeared. That's when she decided to do something. Raisa had the courage to return to Bosnia to help find the men who had sold them into this hell. Tatiana would help put the men in America in prison. That was months ago. Now, in the reality of federal protection, she had second thoughts.

Across the room Gina Crosby sat reading a magazine. Thirty-five years old, she'd joined the FBI after graduating from Cumberland Law School in Birmingham. In the years that followed, she'd investigated hundreds of cases and traveled all over the world. Of everything she'd done, witness protection was her least favorite.

Gina tossed the magazine aside and stood.

"I'll have a look around."

Tatiana stared at the television. Gina disappeared down the hall.

Sometime later there was a knock at the door. Tatiana looked up, suddenly alert. Gina came from the back room. She pulled a pistol from the holster on her hip, glanced through the peephole, then opened the door.

Rita Jackson entered.

"Everything all right?"

Gina glanced outside, then closed the door.

"Yeah." She shoved her pistol into the holster. "Two phone calls. Telemarketer and a wrong number."

"They confirmed the numbers?"

"Yeah." Gina nodded. "It was nothing."

Rita glanced across the room.

"Is she all right?"

Gina shrugged.

"I guess. That's about all she's been doing lately."

Rita shook her head.

"Must have been rough."

Gina nodded.

"I'm sure it was." She slipped on her jacket and turned toward the door. "It's all yours."

Gina stepped outside. Rita closed the door behind her.

Four

*T*he following morning Scott Nolan sat in the conference room at the office of Rankin, Lee and Somerset, a law firm located on the ninth floor of the Tidewater Bank Building in downtown Mobile. Scott rested his hands in his lap and stared down the length of the conference table. Glare from the lights overhead bounced off the polished surface, making his eyes squint and creasing his forehead in a frown. When he'd arrived earlier that morning, the table had seemed as large as the ocean. The room itself had seemed huge and cavernous with its high ceiling and ornate crown molding. He'd even heard a faint echo as the receptionist opened the door. Now, with lawyers crowded around the table and scrunched into every available space, the table and room seemed small and narrow.

Before him, fresh morning faces peered out from a sea of gray suits dotted with patches of white from their shirts and a sprinkling of red from their ties. Not a blue shirt in the crowd. Seeing them there that morning, all neat and tight and wedged in place, brought back memories Scott almost had forgotten.

To his right, tucked out of the way in the corner, was the court reporter. A young, petite blonde, she sat quietly waiting while the men in the room jockeyed for position and slid documents to each other across the table.

Sitting to Scott's left was John Somerset, a middle-aged attorney. Like the others, he wore a gray suit and white shirt starched stiff enough to stand on its own. But, unlike them, he wore a bowtie that, when combined with his round, wire-rimmed glasses, gave him a distinguished, bookish appearance. He was polite but businesslike as he shuffled documents to the others who sat with him

and fielded questions from the men across the table. He was delib-
erate, focused, alert. But there was something else about him that
made him seem not altogether there. He seemed detached but not
exactly, sort of there but not there, engaged but distracted, if possible, all at the same time.

At Somerset's side was his client, Buie Hayford. Easily the
largest man in the room, Hayford had a barrel chest and arms that
bulged against the sleeves of his jacket. Even when he spoke in a
whisper his voice boomed out across the room. He reminded Scott
of a football player. A lineman. A tackle.

Beyond Hayford a rank of stone-faced men lined the left side of
the table. Behind them were more men dressed in the same gray
suits sitting on chairs jammed between the table and door. Out of
the loop of conversation at the table, they busied themselves with
still more documents drawn from the briefcases that sat at their
feet. They flipped through pages, whispered among themselves,
and sipped coffee from Styrofoam cups.

Across the table from Somerset and Hayford sat little Sarah
Braxton. Her strawberry blonde hair was pulled away from her face
and held in place by a pink ribbon. She wore a pink jumper with a
plain white blouse. Scott caught her eye once or twice and tried to
make her smile. She almost did but then looked away and forced
herself to keep a straight face.

Seated beside Sarah was her grandmother, Jessica Stabler.
Slender but not petite, she looked like the matron of a wealthy,
influential family, which she was. And she looked like a woman
who was used to having men do as she pleased. She had keen eyes,
bright but not weak, deep but not mysterious, and her jaw was
always set just so. Scott noticed the way her chin lifted as she spoke
with the men seated around her. He knew that look well and for a
moment thought of his own grandmother, matriarch of the clan,
able to impose her will by nothing but the force of her personality.
A force most often conveyed by what the family referred to as "the
look."

Beside Jessica was Doug Corretti. Approaching seventy-five, he
was a dignified man who looked as though he'd been through these
things a thousand times before. *Unflappable* was the word that
came to Scott's mind. Corretti said very little. While the others
passed their documents and shuffled their papers, he sat with his

hands folded and resting on a blank legal pad that lay on the table before him. When he did speak, it was only a word or two and then only to the man seated next to him—except once when Sarah asked him a question. Then his face lit up and he became rather animated.

The man next to Corretti was Lawrence King. Young and confident, he handled the issues that arose on their side of the table. He passed the papers to their lawyers, answered their questions, and kept order among the ranks of men who sat behind them.

Between the two camps lay the conference table and a lawsuit filed against Buie Hayford and Tidewater National Bank over the manner in which they had administered the Tonsmeyer Family Trust. Millions of dollars and several reputations were up for grabs.

After a few minutes Somerset looked past Scott and caught the court reporter's eye.

She sat up straight and nodded.

"Whenever you're ready."

Five

One floor above, Andre Castille sat on a metal chair and sipped coffee from a plastic cup. The folding table in front of him was covered with electronic gear. Wires ran from the table, snaked across the carpet, and disappeared through a three-foot hole cut in the wall.

Next to Castille was Alan Pate, dressed in blue jeans and a T-shirt. A cigarette dangled from his lips. He adjusted the equipment on the table and slid a pair of headphones over his ears. A moment later he nudged Castille and pointed.

Castille took a pair of headphones from the table and slipped them over his head. The sound of voices from the conference room echoed in his ears.

Pate pressed a button. Reels on a tape recorder began to turn.

Six

Somerset glanced at the legal pad on the table in front of him, took a deep breath, and turned to Scott.

"State your name for the record, please."

"Scott Nolan."

"Is that your full name?"

"Andrew Scott Nolan."

"Where do you live?"

"We have a house on Monterey Street."

"In Mobile?"

"Yes. Mobile, Alabama."

"Tell us your occupation."

"Priest."

"And where are you a priest?"

"St. Pachomius Church."

"That's the church behind the courthouse?"

"Yes."

"Wonderful old building."

"Yes, it is."

"That's an Episcopal church?"

"Yes."

"Rev. Nolan, are you—"

Scott interrupted.

"Most of my parishioners call me Father Scott."

"All right. Father Scott, we're here today about a lawsuit that has been filed against the bank, Tidewater Bank, by Mrs. Jessica Stabler on behalf of her granddaughter, Sarah Braxton, over the way a trust was handled. The Tonsmeyer Family Trust. It was managed by Tidewater Bank. They dispute the manner in which it was managed." Somerset ran his fingers over his lips. "I'm going to ask you some questions today about this case. If you don't understand my question, ask me and I'll be glad to clarify it or repeat it for you. Okay?"

Scott nodded.

"Fine."

"The court reporter is real good at getting everything down, but she can't do a good job with gestures and nods. So I need you to give me a verbal response to the questions. And we need you to speak up so everyone can hear you."

"Okay."

"Are you familiar with the Tonsmeyer Family Trust?"

"No."

"The trust owns a lot of property around town. Does your church rent from anyone?"

"No."

"Do you personally rent from anyone?"

"No."

Somerset used his pen as a pointer.

"The lady sitting across the table is Jessica Stabler. Do you know Mrs. Stabler?"

"No."

"The young lady next to Mrs. Stabler is her granddaughter, Sarah Braxton. Do you know her?"

"No."

"All right. Next to Mrs. Stabler is one of her lawyers, Doug Corretti. Do you know Mr. Corretti?"

"We've never met. I've read about him a time or two in the newspapers."

"Anything to do with this case?"

"Not that I recall."

"The gentleman next to Mr. Corretti is a man named Larry King. Not the man on TV, but the lawyer. Lawrence T. King. Do you know him?"

"No."

"This gentleman to my left is Buie Hayford. Do you know him?"

"No."

Hayford nudged Somerset and whispered something. Somerset leaned to one side to hear, then turned back to Scott.

"Mr. Hayford says he's been to your church a time or two. Do you recall seeing him there?"

Scott shook his head.

Somerset pointed to the court reporter.

"We need an answer so the court reporter can take it down."

"Oh. Sorry. No. I don't recall seeing him there."

"On the other side of Mr. Hayford is Mr. Charles Carr. Next to him is Craig Goolsby. They are from the firm of Goolsby, Sisson and Carr. Do you know either of those two gentlemen? They represent Tidewater Bank in this case."

"No. I don't know them."

"Look around the room. It's kind of full, but do the best you can. Do you see anyone in this room you recognize?"

Scott scanned the room.

"No."

"Sure?"

Scott shook his head.

Somerset pointed to the court reporter once more.

"She needs a response."

"Sorry. No. I don't recognize anyone."

"Ever do any business with Tidewater National Bank?"

"No."

"Does your church?"

"No. As far as I know, we don't."

"Okay. Father Scott, are you married?"

"Yes."

"What is your wife's name?"

"Maggie."

"What was her maiden name?"

"Boatwright. Maggie Boatwright. Margaret Winstead Boatwright."

"Winstead was a family name?"

"Yes."

"Is she from around here?"

"No. She was born in Atlanta, Georgia."

"Where did you meet her?"

"We met in school. University of Mississippi. Oxford, Mississippi."

"Do you or she have any relatives around here?"

"No."

"Have any children?"

"Yes."

"How many do you have?"

"Two."

"Do they live around here?"

"No."

"Where do they live? What cities?"

"They both live in Atlanta."

"What are their names?"

Scott felt the hair on the back of his neck bristle. For some reason he couldn't quite describe, he didn't like the question.

Somerset looked up.

"Your children. What are their names?"

"I ... You know, I'm not going to tell you."

Somerset had a condescending look.

"It's just their names. Their last names."

"They have nothing to do with this."

"We aren't going to talk to them."

Scott glanced around the room. Everyone stared at him. Something inside told him he shouldn't answer. The looks on their faces said he should. Finally, he gave in.

"Standifer." He sighed. "My daughter's last name is Standifer."

"Spell it."

"S-T-A-N-D-I-F-E-R."

"And your son?"

"Nolan. N-O-L-A-N."

Laughter teetered across the room. Somerset glanced around.

"Hey. You never know."

Seven

From deep in a dream Tatiana felt someone shake her shoulder. She rolled over and pulled the covers around her neck. There was another nudge, this one harder than the first. Tatiana opened her eyes.

Sunlight coming through the bedroom window cast a glare across the room. She squinted and rolled on her back. Gina Crosby stared down at her.

"Better get up. They'll be here soon."

Tatiana groaned and closed her eyes. Questions. Always more questions. Every day someone came with questions.

"Why do they want to see me again? I've told them everything a thousand times."

"They want to go over part of your testimony again." Gina shook Tatiana's foot. "Come on. Get up."

Tatiana opened her eyes.

"They think I am lying?"

"No. They just want to make sure they understand." Gina pulled back the covers. "Come on. Better get in the shower."

Tatiana swung her feet from the bed to the floor and rolled into a sitting position. She rested her elbows on her knees and propped her face in her hands.

"They've heard it many times." She ran her fingers through her hair. "Don't they remember what I said?"

"These are new people."

Tatiana didn't like it. She looked up at Gina, her eyes now wide and alert.

"You know these people?"

"I know the agent."

"Someone else is coming with him?"

"Yes."

"What part do they want to talk about?"

"I don't know." Gina placed her hand on Tatiana's shoulder. "Come on. The shower awaits you."

Tatiana stood.

"How many are coming?"

"Just two."

"Who are they?"

"Keith Calhoun from our Jacksonville office. And Byron McCook."

Tatiana frowned.

"Byron The Cook?"

Gina grinned.

"Byron McCook. He's a lawyer. With the U.S. Attorney's office in Mobile."

"You know him?"

Gina shook her head.

"I don't work over there. Come on. You'll feel better after a shower. They'll be here soon."

Tatiana stood by the bed, thinking. Gina gestured toward the bathroom door. Tatiana started in that direction.

Eight

*L*ater that morning Perry Braxton and John Glover met in the parking lot behind Buie Hayford's office. Glover was waiting as Braxton climbed from his car.

"You're late."

"Overslept."

Glover frowned.

"Looks like you've been up all night. Where's your jacket?"

Braxton had a blank look.

"Jacket?"

"You're supposed to look like a detective."

"Oh. Yeah. I forgot."

Braxton opened the trunk of the car and took out a rumpled sport coat. He slipped it on and smiled.

"How about this?"

Glover shook his head and turned away.

"Come on. We'll take my car. I'm not riding with you."

Ten minutes later they turned into the parking lot at the Quick Stop, a convenience store on Airline Highway next door to the building where Panama Tan had been located.

Glover switched off the engine and opened the door. Braxton had a puzzled look.

"Why do you think this place can help?"

Glover pointed to the canopy above the gas pumps.

"Security cameras."

Braxton glanced around.

"I don't know. You think they could see anything?"

"One way to find out."

Inside, Braxton approached a young clerk behind the counter.

"I'm Dan Bradley." He reached inside his jacket and flipped out a badge. "We're investigating an incident that happened out here on the service road. We need to see your security tapes."

The clerk looked confused.

"Security tapes?"

Braxton gestured over his shoulder.

"From the cameras outside."

"Uhh ... Yeah. Sure. They're in the office." The clerk stepped away from the counter. "Back here."

They followed him through the store and down a narrow hallway past the soft-drink coolers. In the office the clerk pulled a cardboard box from beneath the desk.

"These are the tapes." He pointed to a cabinet across the room. "There's a VCR in there if you want to look at them." He glanced over at Braxton. "Or did you want to take them with you?"

Glover moved past the clerk.

"Let's see what you have first."

He opened the box and looked inside. Most of the tapes were not labeled. Several of them were cracked. Magnetic tape had been pulled loose from one.

The door out front opened. The clerk turned away.

"I better see who that is."

Braxton moved to the door to watch. Glover opened the cabinet and turned on the VCR.

Nine

After a midmorning break the lawyers trooped back to the conference room. Scott settled into his chair and did his best to get comfortable. When everyone was seated, Somerset turned to him.

"Where were you born?"

"Petal, Mississippi."

"What is your birthday?"

"June 21, 1949."

"Tell us about your education."

"I graduated from Vanderbilt University with a degree in English. Received a law degree from the University of Mississippi. And a master of divinity from Trinity Theological Seminary."

"You're a lawyer?"

"I have a law degree. That's all."

"Are you admitted to practice law anywhere?"

"Not now."

"Did you ever practice law?"

"Yes."

"Where all have you practiced?"

"I was with Jones Vickroy for eight years."

"The firm in Atlanta?"

"Yes."

"They have a number of offices, don't they? New York. Couple of other places?"

"Yes. New York, Boston, Washington. Have one in Los Angeles now."

"Ever work at any of those other offices?"

"No."

"Just Atlanta?"

"Just Atlanta."

"Ever work as a lawyer anywhere else? Any other firm? On your own?"

"No."

"You were admitted to practice in Georgia?"

"Yes."

"Any other states?"

"Mississippi. Georgia and Mississippi."

"But not now."

"No. I'm not admitted to the bar in any state now."

"Did you ever practice law in Mississippi?"

"No."

"Ever try a case in Mississippi?"

"No."

"Ever represent any Mississippi clients in any matter?"

"No."

"Ever take a deposition in Mississippi?"

"No. I don't think so."

"But you had a Mississippi license?"

"I had a Mississippi license because that's where I went to school. That's where my family lived. Thought it would be a good warm-up for the Georgia bar exam. And in the back of my mind I thought I might one day move back to Mississippi."

"Where in Mississippi does your family live?"

"All over. I grew up in Petal. My grandfather lived in Wiggins. My other grandfather lived in Magee. Cousins all over."

"Any down here, in Mobile County?"

"No."

"Just to make sure, what was the grandfather's name? The one in Wiggins."

"Nolan. Roscoe Nolan."

"His first name was Roscoe?"

"Not really. That's what his friends called him. His real name was Henry. Winston Henry Nolan III."

"And the one in Magee?"

"Meadows. Hilburn Meadows."

"All right. Ever try any cases in Alabama?"

"No."

"You knew when you graduated from law school you were

going to Jones Vickroy?"

"Yes."

"Work during the summers while you were in law school?"

"Yes."

"Where?"

"The first summer I worked for Allen and Daniels, a firm in Jackson."

"Mississippi?"

"Yes. The next summer I was with Jones Vickroy."

"In Atlanta?"

"Yes."

"Hold any clerkships along the way?"

"No."

"Went straight from law school to Jones Vickroy?"

"Yes."

"What kind of work did you do? As a lawyer."

"I worked in the insurance defense section. Spent most of my time figuring out ways for insurance companies to keep the money they should have been paying in claims."

"Not a bad business."

"Maybe."

From down the table Charles Carr spoke up.

"Object to the form of the question."

Somerset gestured toward Carr.

"Mr. Carr's firm has a large insurance defense practice."

Scott smiled. Somerset continued.

"What was your position there? At Jones Vickroy."

"I was an associate."

"Senior associate?"

"Jones Vickroy didn't have senior associates. Just associates and partners."

"Eight years and you didn't make partner?"

"I was about to."

"What happened?"

"I went to a movie."

"A movie?"

"Yes."

"You just checked out one day, went to a movie, and they fired you?"

"Not exactly. I didn't leave the office to go to a movie. And they didn't fire me. I quit."

"To become a priest?"

"Not right away."

"What did you do between being an associate at Jones Vickroy and becoming a priest?"

"I went to a movie."

"A movie?"

"A movie. And seminary."

"What was the name of that movie?"

"*The Matrix*."

Someone laughed out loud. Somerset frowned.

"I've heard of it. I think. Never saw it. How did you wind up at this movie?"

"My son wanted to see it. My wife and daughter were out of town. He and I went."

"And because of this movie, you became a priest?"

"It was an eye-opening experience."

Ten

*T*atiana stood at the sliding glass door and gazed down at the swimming pool in the courtyard below. She sipped a cup of coffee and watched as a woman dove into the pool and swam to the shallow end.

Gina took her by the arm.

"I've told you before." She pulled Tatiana back to the center of the room. "If you want to look outside in the daytime, stand back here. No one can see you here."

Tatiana pulled free of her grasp.

"But I can't see the pool from back there."

"If you stand at the door, they can see you."

"Who can see me?"

"Anyone can see you."

Tatiana turned away.

"You don't even know if there is someone out there looking for me."

Gina relaxed.

"They're out there, Tatiana. But if you follow the rules, they'll never find you."

"For how long?"

Gina frowned.

"How long?"

"Yes. For how long do I follow the rules? Can't go out. Can't take a walk." She gestured toward the glass door. "Can't go for a swim. Can't look at someone swimming. How long?"

Gina had a somber look.

"For as long as the threat exists."

Tatiana shook her head.

"This is not a life."
"But you are alive."
"No. I am a bird in a cage."

Eleven

At noon Hayford returned to his office.

Castille was waiting for him. "Can't he move a little faster?"

Hayford sighed.

"That's just Somerset being Somerset. He starts asking questions, and then he wants to know everything." Hayford dropped onto the chair behind his desk. "Might be helpful. I don't know." He looked over at Castille. "Get anything out of it besides the daughter's last name?"

"No. Not really."

"Think you can do anything with that?"

"Yeah. We can find her. Shouldn't take too long. I have a couple of guys working on it."

"Good."

Castille took a seat across from the desk.

"What about Braxton and Glover? Did they find anything yet?"

Hayford rolled his eyes.

"Not yet. I should have left Perry out of it. He can't keep his head on straight long enough to do any good. They went to a convenience store over there by where the tanning salon used to be. The clerk let them see the tapes from the security camera, but they only keep them for three months."

"What do they do with the old ones?"

"Tape over them, I think."

Castille nodded his head.

"If we had them, we might be able to do something with them. They still use videotape?"

"That's what Glover said."

"Lot of these places have digital systems now. Dump all that stuff on a disk. You can store years' worth without any trouble."

"Yeah, well, this wasn't one of those places." Hayford gently rocked the chair. "I told Glover to keep working on it by himself. Not to worry about waiting around for Perry."

"I have someone in Atlanta who might be able to get us the priest's file from Jones Vickroy."

Hayford leaned back in his chair.

"You think there's anything in it that would help us find the girl?"

"I don't know. With this kind of thing, you never know what will lead you to where you want to be. We take everything we can find, plug it into a computer program, run it through a bunch of different matrixes. There's no telling what we'll find when we cross it all up."

Hayford smiled.

Castille gave him a look. "What are you grinning about?"

"Matrix."

Castille shrugged. "Whatever." He stood. "Look, I got a guy working on the priest's other accounts. He has a ..." He stopped short, an odd look on his face. "You sure you want to know about all this?"

Hayford laced his fingers together behind his head and leaned back further in the chair.

"Andre, if we don't find that girl, they're going to put me away for the rest of my life. What do I care about stealing a few credit card files?"

Twelve

All morning Tatiana sat at the dining table with Keith Calhoun and Byron McCook, answering question after question about what she'd seen. Who was there. What they'd said. By lunch she'd had enough. She leaned forward and rested her head on the table.

Gina spoke up.

"Hey, look at that. It's one o'clock. Anybody hungry?"

Tatiana lifted her head and grumbled.

"No more turkey sandwiches."

Gina smiled.

"What about a hamburger?"

Tatiana's eyes brightened.

"McDonald's?"

"Sure." Gina glanced over at Calhoun. "Keith, why don't you run down the street and get us all a Big Mac."

Calhoun stood.

"I could use the exercise."

McCook leaned back from the table.

"Make mine a Cobb salad."

Calhoun left the apartment. McCook looked over at Tatiana.

"You know, this part is very important. The part where you saw them together. We have to be sure we all understand what you saw."

Tatiana frowned. McCook explained.

"This isn't just some criminal we're going after. He's a powerful man. He has friends in high places. It's critical that we understand the exact sequence of events in that condo. Who was there. Where they were. What they said and did." He looked Tatiana in the eye. "Exactly."

Tatiana didn't like the tone of his voice. He wasn't talking to some little girl. She stood.

"You think I am lying."

"No. I don't, but—"

She cut him off.

"Yes, you do. I can see it in your eyes. You don't think I'm telling you the truth. You wouldn't keep going over and over the same thing if you did."

McCook folded his hands behind his head.

"No. I do, but ..."

Tatiana slapped the back of the chair.

"Something has changed." Her eyes darted from McCook to Gina and back again. "Something has changed." She pointed a finger at McCook. "Tell me what it is."

McCook sighed and looked away. Tatiana pressed the point.

"What? What is it? Why won't you tell me? Is it *your* life you are putting on the line?" She answered her own question. "No. It's not. So why won't you tell me?" She leaned over the chair. "What has changed?"

McCook didn't respond. Tatiana came around the chair and leaned over the table, her face just inches from his.

"Tell me, or we are through."

McCook glanced at Gina, then back to Tatiana.

"We've received some calls from Washington on this."

Gina leaned forward.

"You've received some calls?"

McCook stood.

"Listen, I don't like it, but that's the way these things work."

Gina leaned back in her chair.

"Well, that's just great, Byron. We get all the way into this, and now everyone wants to cover their careers." She rose from her chair. "You worried about your career, Byron? Is that what this is about? Wonder if you're going to make that next pay grade?"

McCook shoved his hands in his pockets.

"I'm not the one calling the shots on this. I just go where I'm told and do what they say."

Gina nodded.

"Like I said, covering your career."

McCook leaned away.

"Look, no one's backing out. But everyone wants to make sure the story will hold."

Tatiana threw up her hands.

"They think I'm lying."

McCook's face turned red. He jabbed his finger at her. "No one thinks you're lying." He moved closer to her. "Listen to me, there is an office full of people who are putting their careers on the line for this. This isn't something that will win anyone a promotion, but it's the right thing to do and we are doing it. So stop saying we think you're lying." He looked over at Gina and lowered his voice. "But if we're going out on this limb, we want to make sure it'll hold. That's all. We want to make sure the story will hold."

Thirteen

The following morning everyone took their places around the conference table at Somerset's office. When they were seated and ready, Somerset picked up where he'd left off the day before.

"Now, Father Scott, tell us about your work history."

"Where do I begin?"

"How about the beginning?"

"Okay. My first job was picking watermelons the summer I turned twelve."

Somerset interrupted with a wave of his hand.

"That's all right. Begin with your first full-time job. Maybe after college."

"In college I worked as a busboy and then as a waiter. After I graduated, I took a job as a graduate instructor in the English department at Vanderbilt. Thought about pursuing a doctorate in English. Worked on it about a year and then went to law school."

"What brought you to that choice?"

"My father was an attorney. Actually I think he's still a member of the bar."

"He's still alive?"

"Yes. He's ninety-two."

"Any other lawyers in your family?"

"Not now. My father's father, my grandfather, was a judge in Wiggins. Stone County."

"They both have the same last name? Nolan?"

"Yes."

"So, continuing with your work history. You went to Ole Miss law school."

"Yes. Then Jones Vickroy recruited me to clerk for them the

summer after my second year. They made me an offer that fall. I went with them after graduation. Stayed there eight years."

"You left Jones Vickroy. Then what?"

"I left Jones Vickroy and enrolled at Trinity Theological Seminary. It's in Alexandria, Virginia."

"Work anywhere while you were there?"

"No."

"Where'd you go after seminary?"

"After seminary I—"

Somerset held up his hand.

"Just a minute."

Hayford whispered in Somerset's ear. Somerset frowned and shook his head.

"I'm sorry. Please continue. After seminary?"

"After I graduated, I went to a church in Corsicana, Texas. Was there as an associate for two years, then went to Kingston, Texas, as the rector at St. Bartholomew. Then to St. Pachomius here in Mobile."

"How did you get from seminary to the first church in Texas?"

"The bishop of that diocese came to the seminary. He had a couple of openings. Suggested I might fit at Corsicana. I went down. Talked to them. They hired me."

"And how did you get from there to the church in Kingston?"

"They sent a search committee to see me."

"St. Bartholomew's recruited you to be their rector?"

"Yes."

"And, just for the record, what is a rector?"

"A priest. The head priest. The priest in charge of a parish. A typical parish."

"There are other heads of other parishes that aren't known as rectors?"

"Yes. But it doesn't have anything to do with what you're here about. I mean, the rector of the bishop's official parish is called the dean. Things like that."

"Okay. Now you were in Corsicana for two years. How long were you at Kingston?"

"Three years."

"Two years at the first church. Three years at the second. Five years in the ministry, and you come to a large downtown church in Mobile, Alabama. How did that happen?"

"Well, it wasn't a large church when I came here. They were running about sixty on Sunday mornings. They had some well-known members, but in terms of numbers they were smaller than either of the two churches I had been at before."

"How did it work? You coming here. Another search committee came looking for you?"

"Yes. Our first year at Corsicana we attended a conference in Galveston. Met some people from Destin, Florida. The rector at Destin is a priest named Alan Armstrong. We met him and his wife. Over the years we spent a couple of vacations at their house in Destin. They would go out of town on vacation. We took our vacation at the same time and stayed at their house. Alan knows a lot of people along the Gulf Coast. When St. Pachomius started looking for a new priest, he mentioned my name."

"Did someone from Mobile come to Texas to talk to you?"

"Yes. Alan told them about me. They sent me a letter asking if I was interested in considering the position. Then three of their members came out to see me."

"Who came to see you?"

"Their names?"

"Yes."

"Frank Parker, Carson Rockett, and Wick Skinner."

"Carson Rockett?"

The court reporter interrupted.

"Spell that name, please."

Scott turned to her.

"R-O-C-K-E-T-T."

Somerset continued.

"And the other one? Wick?"

"Wick Skinner. Actually, his name is Wycliff. W-Y-C-L-I-F-F. Last name is S-K-I-N-N-E-R."

"So these three men came to see you."

"Yes."

"And then what? What happened?"

"They came on Friday night. We talked and visited Saturday. They came to church on Sunday morning. We went to lunch. They went home."

"Did they offer you the job that weekend?"

"No. They had one other candidate to look at. But they passed on him and hired me."

"And you've been there how long?"

"At St. Pachomius?"

"Yes."

"About ten years."

Fourteen

*T*hat afternoon Glover stopped by Hayford's office. Hayford was standing near his desk as Glover entered.

"You have class tonight?"

Glover nodded.

"Did Perry show up this afternoon?"

"I don't know. You'd have to ask Castille. Anything new on finding a picture?"

Glover shook his head.

"I checked everywhere I could think of that might have a camera."

"Nothing?"

"Nothing."

"What about Perry?"

Glover scoffed.

"He's useless."

"Did he go with you this morning?"

"Yeah. He was there."

Hayford took a seat at his desk. Glover moved farther into the room.

"You got any other ideas?"

Hayford looked away, thinking. After a moment he looked up at Glover.

"Emerald Coast Condos." He sighed. "You remember what she looked like?"

Glover grinned.

"I remember."

Fifteen

At nine o'clock the following morning Scott was seated once again in the chair at the conference table. Somerset took a mint from his pocket and slipped it into his mouth.

"Now do you know one Mike Connolly? I think his full name is John Michael Connolly Jr."

Scott laced his fingers together and rested his hands in his lap. "Yes."

"How do you know him?"

"He is a member of my church. St. Pachomius."

"When did you first become acquainted with him?"

"About ... four or five years ago."

"How did you come to know Mr. Connolly?"

"He came to the church one day to talk to me."

"Tell us about the first time you met him."

"Not much to tell. He came to the church one afternoon, wanted to ask me about one of our members."

"Who was that? Which member?"

The question made Scott uncomfortable, but he couldn't think of a reason not to answer.

"Keyton Attaway."

The expression on Somerset's face softened.

"I remember Keyton. Didn't realize he went to your church. Why was Mr. Connolly asking about him?"

"He came to see me after Keyton ... was killed. He was defending a man arrested for murdering him."

"Mr. Connolly was defending the man the police accused of murdering Keyton Attaway?"

"Yes."

"What happened? When he came to see you that first time?"

"As best I can remember, it was late one afternoon. I don't know the exact date. We talked briefly. He wanted to know if I knew anything that might explain why someone would want to kill Keyton."

"What did you tell him?"

"I told him no, I didn't know why, but that he was upset the last several times I saw him."

"Who was upset?"

"Keyton."

"You told Mr. Connolly you thought Keyton Attaway was upset?"

"Yes."

"Did the police question you about Keyton Attaway?"

"No."

"Did anyone else talk to you about this? About Keyton Attaway? After he was killed? After Keyton Attaway was murdered, did anyone else talk to you about him? I don't mean your church members just talking. I mean, did anyone else question you about him?"

"Yes."

"Who?"

"Right after Mike came to see me, another guy came by. I don't know his name."

"You mean he came in that same day?"

"Yes."

"As Mr. Connolly was leaving?"

"Almost. He was waiting for me by my car. Asked me some questions about Mike. About Keyton."

"What kinds of questions?"

"They have nothing to do with any of this case you have going here."

"What kinds of questions did this person ask you?"

"They weren't really questions. More like statements. Like he was telling me. He was asking me questions, but the whole point was to tell me things. It was a ... It was a lot of nonsense."

"What did he ask you?"

"He wanted to know if I knew about Mike's problems with alcohol."

"Did you?"

"Not really."

"What does that mean?"

"We hadn't talked about it at that point."

"But you knew."

"I guess."

"How? How did you know Mr. Connolly had a problem with alcohol?"

"When we talked, I thought I smelled it."

"Smelled what?"

"Alcohol."

"You smelled alcohol on his breath?"

"Yes. I guess. Not really on his breath. More like just on him."

"So when this guy suggested Mr. Connolly might have a problem with alcohol, you weren't surprised."

"I wasn't surprised that Mike might have a problem. I was surprised that he would mention it to me."

"What else did he ask about?"

"Wanted to know if I knew anything about Mike Connolly's drug habit."

"Did you?"

Scott shook his head.

"He doesn't have a drug habit."

"You know that now?"

"Yes."

"Did you know that then?"

"I didn't know much about him at all then. I'd only seen him that one time."

"But in that one meeting you suspected he had a problem with alcohol."

"I knew he'd had a drink sometime that day, before he came to see me. I wondered if he had a problem."

"Did this man who asked you about him, did he tell you his name?"

"No."

"Did he ask you any other questions?"

"Not really questions. Like I said, they were more like statements."

"Such as?"

"He let me know that Keyton Attaway was friends with some important people."

"Like?"

"Truman Albritton. Hogan Smith. He might have mentioned a few others."

"You knew Truman Albritton?"

"I knew he was a lawyer."

"And Hogan Smith. Senator Hogan Smith?"

"Yes."

"How did you know that's who he was referring to?"

"He told me. He said Keyton was a well-connected guy. That it was a terrible loss. Horrible thing for some guy to do to him, for just a watch and a few dollars. That was all Keyton had on him. A few dollars and a watch. A well-connected guy like him, dying for a watch and pocket change. That's exactly what he said, 'dying for a watch and pocket change.'"

"Did he say why he was there? Why he was asking you these questions?"

"No. But I had a pretty good idea."

"Why did you think he was telling you this?"

"He was there to tell me to be careful about what I said to Mike Connolly about Keyton Attaway."

"He told you that?"

"Not in so many words. But that was the point of it."

"Had you ever seen this man before?"

"No."

"Have you seen him since?"

"No."

"Did you ever tell anyone about him?"

"No. Not that I recall."

"Well, I need you to recall. Ever tell Mr. Connolly about him?"

"No."

"Ever tell the police about him?"

"No."

"Ever tell Hollis Toombs about him?"

"No."

"You know Hollis Toombs?"

"Yes."

"We'll get to him in a little while. Ever talk to your wife about this man? Your secretary? Another parishioner?"

"No."

"Who else talked to you about Keyton or about Mr. Connolly? There around the time of Keyton's death."

"His wife talked to me several times."

"Mr. Connolly's wife?"

"No. Keyton's wife. Karen. Karen Attaway."

"Anyone else besides her?"

"An insurance adjuster came to see me."

"What did he want?"

"From what he said, Keyton must have had a large insurance policy. Said he was just doing some checking since a claim had been filed on the policy. Wanted to know if Keyton was depressed, that sort of thing."

"They thought he killed himself?"

"They didn't want to pay the claim."

"For what reason? Did he tell you they didn't want to pay?"

"It was obvious that's why he was investigating. They didn't have a reason not to pay. But they were looking for one."

"In your opinion. Now—"

"No. I know what he was doing. I've done it myself."

"You did what?"

"As an attorney. Insured with a huge life insurance policy dies. They want to find out what the story is behind it before they pay out the death benefit."

"Was this a policy he had recently taken out?"

"I don't know. I don't know anything about it other than that guy came and talked to me."

"And from that you surmised that Mr. Attaway had a large policy. A policy with a large death benefit."

"Yes."

"Ever hear anyone say whether that policy was paid?"

"No."

"Anyone else talk to you, question you, about Keyton Attaway or Mike Connolly? At that time."

"No."

"You look like there's more to it than that."

Scott shrugged.

"There was one guy. At a party."

"Who?"

"Frank Ingram."

"Ingram Shipbuilding?"

"Yes."

"You knew him?"

"I know his father. We were at a party. A birthday party. Tootsie Trehern's birthday party. Joe was there."

"Joe?"

"Joe Ingram. He was there. Introduced me to his son. Frank. Sometime later I was talking to someone else. Frank was standing there. He said he'd heard Keyton belonged to my church. That he and I were good friends. What did I know about Mike Connolly."

"Frank Ingram asked you this?"

"Yes."

"Did he say anything else?"

"I thought it was odd that he knew I knew about Keyton. Frank isn't a member of our church. I didn't remember seeing him at the funeral. So, anyway, he started talking about how well-known Keyton was and how many friends he had and how they were all these powerful people. Judge Agostino. Hogan Smith. People who had power and could really move things. And then he started asking about Mike Connolly."

"What did he ask about Mr. Connolly?"

"Well, he didn't really ask. See, that's the thing. Just like that other guy. It wasn't like he was questioning me, really. More like he was telling me things. He said he'd heard Mike had a problem with alcohol. Said everybody knew that. Said somebody'd told him Mike was using pills."

"Somebody told Frank that Mike was using pills?"

"Yes. That's what he said."

"Did he say who told him that?"

"No. It was just one of those party conversation comments. 'Somebody said this.' 'Somebody said that.' The kind of thing you don't attribute to anyone so you don't have to hear about it when someone finds out you were saying what they'd said. 'Somebody said.' That's all."

"What else did he say?"

"He was asking me did I know that. How could a guy like that defend anyone charged with a crime? If that was the best the guy could do, he must be guilty."

"Who must be guilty?"

"The man they'd arrested for killing Keyton. If Mike was the best he could do for an attorney, he must be guilty."

"And this conversation bothered you?"

"Yes. I mean, at that point I'd had maybe one or two conversations with Mike." Scott's voice grew louder and he gestured with his hands as he spoke. "And now two people I'd never met before are asking me about him and telling me what a great guy Keyton was and how powerful his friends were and what a lush Mike Connolly was."

"Sounds like it made you mad."

"I don't know about mad." Scott's shoulders slumped. "Well ... yeah. It made me a little angry." He smiled. "That they would jump on this guy. I mean, I didn't know Mike at that point, but he didn't seem like the villain in the thing, either. And here they were slandering the guy, and all he was doing was trying to defend his client."

"Anyone else question you about Keyton Attaway or Mike Connolly?"

"No."

"How did Mr. Connolly find you? What made him think to ask you about Keyton?"

"There was a cross in Keyton's office that I had given him. I think he saw it."

"Mr. Connolly had been in Keyton's office?"

"Yes."

"Were they friends?"

"I don't know. I think they knew each other."

"When was he in Keyton's office?"

"I don't know."

"Sometime after the murder, but before he came to see you?"

"Probably."

"Did he tell you that?"

"No. I just assumed he'd seen it since the murder."

"Now earlier you said you thought Mr. Attaway was upset in the weeks leading up to his murder. Why did you think Mr. Attaway was upset? "

"From the way he acted."

"You had seen Mr. Attaway in the days prior to his murder?"

"Yes."

"Work backwards from his death and tell me when you saw him."

Goolsby spoke up.

"What does this have to do with our lawsuit?"

"Just taking a deposition." Somerset continued. "Work backwards from Keyton's murder and tell me when you saw him in those weeks leading up to his death. When did he die? What day of the week was it?"

"He died on a Wednesday afternoon, I think."

"How did you hear about his death?"

"Brett Davis called me."

"Who is Brett Davis?"

"He's one of our members. He and Keyton were good friends. Brett called me and told me about it. I went down to Keyton's house as soon as I hung up the phone."

"What does Brett Davis do? Where does he work?"

"He's in construction."

"Who does he work for?"

"He's in business for himself."

"Ever see him with Keyton Attaway?"

"Yes. Many times."

"Where have you seen him with Keyton Attaway?"

"Church. Keyton's house. Once or twice at Brett's."

"When was the next time you saw Keyton Attaway? Before that Wednesday when you found out he was dead."

"I had seen him the Sunday before that. He was at church. And ... I know we went fishing that Saturday."

"The Saturday before the Wednesday he died?"

"Yes. I'm just trying to make sure if I saw him any other times after that. I know I saw him that next day. Sunday. But I don't think I saw him again before he died."

"So you and he went fishing?"

"Yes."

"What did you talk about while you were fishing?"

"I'm not going to tell you that."

"Excuse me?"

"That would be privileged communication. Between a priest and parishioner."

"Was it penitential in nature?"

"It's privileged."

Larry King tossed his pen on the table.

"Here we go."

Charles Carr leaned around the man beside him and glanced down the table.

"John, let's go off the record a minute."

Somerset shook his head.

"No. I'm entitled to an answer. Either he gives me the answer or he tells me why he can't."

Scott responded.

"I can't answer because the conversation you are asking about is privileged communication."

Sixteen

By ten o'clock that morning Glover was in Orange Beach, a resort town along the coast near the Alabama-Florida line. He turned from the highway into the parking lot at Emerald Coast Condos and parked near the front entrance.

Inside, he made his way to the check-in desk. A young brunette smiled at him from behind the counter.

"May I help you?"

"My name is Steve Shaw. My grandmother was down here visiting someone ..."

He noticed the girl behind the counter was wearing shorts with an Auburn University logo on the leg.

"Do you go to Auburn?"

She smiled.

"I did last semester. Do you?"

"No. I'm in law school."

"Wow. Where?"

Glover gave her a pained expression.

"Alabama."

She nodded.

"Not much choice, I guess."

"Not really. Unless you want to go to Cumberland."

She smiled and giggled. He grinned and did his best to look interested.

"Look, my grandmother was down here visiting a friend. At least that's what she says she was doing. No one is really sure where she was. She's kind of not really thinking very well."

The girl nodded. Glover continued.

"But it's really important for us to put her with that friend that weekend, if that's where she was." He leaned over the counter and lowered his voice. "Do you think you could let me see the video from your security cameras for that weekend she was down here?"

"When was it?"

"Last year. In June."

The girl frowned.

"Last year?"

Glover nodded. The girl gave him a disbelieving look.

"Are you sure she was your grandmother?"

"Yeah. I'm not lying."

"I don't know."

Glover put up his hands.

"If I was lying, I wouldn't have told you I was at Alabama."

Her eyes sparkled. He grinned even wider.

"I'm telling you the truth. She was down here to see a friend." Glover paused and dropped his head. "Okay. If we're being honest." He gave her a sheepish look. "It was a guy, okay? I mean, if what she said was true, it was a guy. That's what she says. She's almost eighty years old, it's hard to imagine, but she says she was down here with some guy for the weekend."

The girl grinned.

"Nothing wrong with that."

Glover shook his head.

"No. You're right. I guess she can do whatever she wants to. After all, she's Grandma. But half the family thinks she's lying and the other half thinks this man she was with is just some guy trying to take advantage of her. So." Glover cocked his head to one side. "Think you still have videos that far back?"

She glanced over her shoulder, as if checking to see who was around, then gestured for him to follow.

"I don't think I'm supposed to do this." She looked over her shoulder once more. "But come back here." There was a mischievous look in her eye. "I think they keep those in a closet back here." She giggled. "I hope no one finds out."

She led him into an office and closed the door.

Seventeen

When Scott refused to answer Somerset's questions, the deposition ended early. Somerset spent the afternoon catching up on work that had accumulated in his office. By lunch he had filed a motion asking the court to force Scott to answer. A sheriff's deputy served Scott with a notice of the hearing.

Faced with appearing in court, Scott called Mike Connolly. Connolly referred him to Greg Collins. Scott arranged to meet with him that evening. Collins was waiting for him as he entered the office.

"Father Scott, come on in."

They started down the hall.

"It's just you and me here. Everyone else has already gone home. You want something to drink?"

Scott shook his head.

"No, thank you."

Collins guided him to an office and pointed to a chair across the room from the desk.

"Let's sit over here."

A pair of upholstered armchairs sat near a window. They took a seat. Collins crossed his legs.

"So John Somerset wants you to tell him about a conversation you had with Keyton Attaway?"

"Yeah. Can they force me to tell them about it?"

Collins shrugged.

"Depends on the nature of the conversation."

"He wants to know about a fishing trip."

Collins had a skeptical look.

"Might be tough to keep that out."

"You think?"

"I checked with the clerk's office. That case is set before Judge McKenzie."

"What's she like?"

Collins smiled.

"Sarah Katherine McKenzie. I went to law school with her. Nice lady. Smart."

"Think that'll help?"

"That I went to law school with her?"

"Yes."

Collins shrugged.

"I doubt it. She's about as honest as she is smart. She'd be more sympathetic to you, as a priest, than she would to me. With me she'd just be slamming a law school friend. With you she might feel like she was putting God in jail." He chuckled. "She might have second thoughts about that."

Scott bounced his leg on the ball of his foot.

"I'm not sure why they want to know about this fishing trip. Not much happened."

Collins nodded.

"Tell me about that conversation."

Eighteen

That evening Hayford sat at his desk reading through a transcript of Scott's testimony. Glover appeared at the door. Hayford glanced up.

"What are you grinning about?"

Glover came from the door and took a seat in front of the desk.

"You look tired. Have a rough day?"

Hayford returned to the transcript lying on the desk. His head was bent over it, his eyes focused on the page.

"Somerset has us bogged down in a shouting match with the priest."

"Over what?"

"Something that doesn't really matter."

"Who's going to win?"

Hayford turned the page.

"We'll find out in a few days."

"He filed a motion to compel?"

"Yes."

"Hearing scheduled yet?"

"Yes."

Glover leaned to one side in the chair and slouched against the armrest.

"What's the problem?"

"Conversation with Keyton Attaway."

"The priest doesn't want to talk about it?"

"No."

"Can't you just work around it?"

Hayford shook his head.

"Deposition's on hold."

"For how long?"

"Until we get before Judge McKenzie."

"She couldn't hear it today?"

"I guess not."

Hayford turned another page of the transcript. Glover brushed lint from his shirtsleeve.

"Seems like this would be a priority."

"She's in the middle of a trial."

Hayford took off his glasses and shoved the transcript aside. When he looked up he finally noticed the look on Glover's face.

"You seem pleased at yourself. What's up?"

Glover reached into his pocket and pulled out a photograph. He leaned forward, half out of the chair, and dropped the picture on the desk.

"Look familiar?"

He slid back in the chair. Hayford picked up the photo. His eyes grew wide with surprise.

"Where'd you get ..." He stared at the photo, his mouth agape. "That's her."

Glover grinned and nodded. Hayford laughed and pointed to the picture.

"That's her." He looked over at Glover. "Where'd you find this?"

Glover had a satisfied smile.

"The condo."

Hayford frowned.

"The condo?"

"Emerald Coast. You told me about it the other day."

"And they actually had the tapes from that far back?"

Glover nodded. Hayford pointed at the picture again.

"That was a break. How about that?" He laid the photograph on the desk. "How'd you get them to let you look at the tapes?"

Glover gave a nonchalant tip of his head.

"You know, a smile, a few words ... a weekend at Auburn, you can get anything."

Hayford chuckled.

"Weekend at Auburn? Not this weekend. You'll be spending your time on the road."

Glover's smile vanished.

"The road? Where?"

Hayford opened a humidor that sat near the corner of the desk. He took out a cigar and leaned back in his chair.

"Marianna, Florida, for starters."

Deep furrows wrinkled Glover's forehead.

"Marianna? Where is that?"

Hayford clipped the end off the cigar and took a box of matches from the desk drawer.

"Just a minute and I'll tell you."

Nineteen

Two days later the lawyers gathered in Judge McKenzie's courtroom. Somerset and Hayford sat at the counsel table to the left of the bench. Scott and Greg Collins sat at the table to the right. Judge McKenzie looked down at the file lying on her desk.

"We are here today on defendant Buie Hayford's motion to compel answers at the deposition of one Andrew Scott Nolan." She looked up. "Mr. Somerset, you may proceed."

Somerset rose from behind the counsel's table.

"Your Honor, we are prepared for argument, and, if the court would allow, we would like to call a witness."

"I'll hear whatever you have."

"Very well. As the court is aware, I noticed the deposition of Andrew Scott Nolan, who is the rector at St. Pachomius Church. Rev. Nolan appeared for that deposition under subpoena. In the course of that deposition I asked him about a fishing trip he took with one of his parishioners. Rev. Nolan refused to answer my questions about the nature of the conversation he had with that parishioner and asserted that the communication was protected by the priest-penitent privilege, I guess under our Rules of Evidence. That would be Rule 505."

Somerset moved around the table and stood in front of the judge's bench.

"As the court is also aware, I attempted to work out some accommodation with him, but Rev. Nolan continued to refuse. And so I filed my motion."

Judge McKenzie looked around.

"Mr. Collins, are you representing Rev. Nolan in this matter?"

Collins rose from his chair.

"Yes, Your Honor. I am."

"What does your client have to say about this?"

"Your Honor, this deposition was being taken in the course of civil litigation between the Tonsmeyer Family Trust and Tidewater Bank over the way Tidewater and Mr. Hayford handled some of the trust assets. It has nothing to do with any claims against Rev. Nolan or St. Pachomius Church. Neither of them are parties to this matter. The questions posed to Rev. Nolan, to which he refused to respond, addressed a conversation, or conversations, he had with a parishioner with whom he had a long and close relationship. The fact that those conversations took place on a boat, miles out in the Gulf, doesn't negate the privilege."

Judge McKenzie frowned at Somerset.

"What are we talking about here? A conversation about who won the ball game or a conversation about someone's marriage?"

Somerset shrugged.

"That's just it, Your Honor. We don't know because Rev. Nolan wouldn't tell us even the general nature of those conversations."

Collins spoke up.

"Your Honor, Rev. Nolan couldn't divulge the nature of the conversation, not even the topics, without disclosing what they'd talked about. He would have compromised the privilege by doing that."

Judge McKenzie threw up her hands and scooted back in her chair.

"Well, we have to know the nature of those conversations before we can proceed." She turned to the bailiff. "Clear the courtroom."

The bailiff came from his desk beside the bench. Judge McKenzie raised her voice and spoke to the audience.

"Anyone in here not a lawyer on this motion?" She looked across the room. "We need you to step out into the hall for a few minutes, please. Sorry for the inconvenience."

The bailiff started down the aisle toward the door. Somerset turned to face the bench and tried to continue.

"Your Honor, I would like—"

Judge McKenzie cut him off.

"Just a moment, Mr. Somerset. Let's wait until everyone is gone."

When the courtroom was clear of spectators, Judge McKenzie looked at Scott.

"Now, Rev. Nolan, come on up here and take a seat."

Scott made his way around the table to the witness stand. Judge McKenzie turned to face him.

"Raise your right hand, please, sir. Do you swear or affirm the testimony you are about to give is the truth, the whole truth, and nothing but the truth?"

Scott nodded.

"I affirm."

"Very well. Be seated. Mr. Somerset, you may proceed."

Somerset stood in front of Scott.

"State your name for the record, please."

"Andrew Scott Nolan."

"You are the rector at St. Pachomius Church?"

"Yes."

"And you are an ordained and licensed minister?"

"Yes."

"I subpoenaed you to give a deposition in the case of Tonsmeyer Family Trust v. Buie Hayford and Tidewater National Bank, did I not?"

"Yes, you did."

"And you appeared at that deposition as scheduled."

"Yes."

"In the course of taking your deposition, you told me about a fishing trip you took with Keyton Attaway the Saturday before he was murdered."

"Yes."

"He was murdered on Wednesday. You went fishing with him on the Saturday before that Wednesday."

"Yes."

"Where did you leave from?"

"A marina down at Dauphin Island."

"Went out several miles into the Gulf."

"Yes."

Collins stood.

"Your Honor, I object. This is just what we were talking about. This has nothing to do with the case they've filed against Tidewater Bank. The case he's trying to defend."

Judge McKenzie looked at Somerset.

"Mr. Somerset?"

"I'm entitled to lay some context. I think the court would want to know the context of the matters at issue."

"Overruled."

Somerset continued.

"In the course of that trip did you and Keyton Attaway talk to each other?"

"Yes."

"What topics did you talk about?"

"As I told you before, I can't answer that. Those conversations were privileged communication between a priest and his parishioner."

Judge McKenzie turned to face Scott.

"Rev. Nolan, we are here today to test that privilege. If the topics of those conversations fall within the privilege, you won't have to disclose the details of the conversation. Answer the question."

"And if I don't?

"If you don't answer Mr. Somerset's questions this morning, you will go to jail until you do."

"Could I speak to Mr. Collins a moment, Your Honor?"

Judge McKenzie smiled and nodded.

"By all means." She glanced around the courtroom. "We'll take a few minutes." She turned to the bailiff as she left the bench. "Call me when they get ready."

Scott stepped down from the witness stand. Collins came from his chair behind the table and led him down the aisle to the door.

Twenty

Andre Castille turned into an alley off St. Joseph Street and brought the car to a stop. A door from the building to the left opened, and a woman appeared. As she started toward the car, Castille lowered the window. She nervously glanced around and handed him a brown envelope.

Castille pressed a wad of cash against her palm. She turned away and disappeared inside the building. Castille tossed the envelope on the seat beside him and drove up the alley.

Ten minutes later he turned off Spring Hill Avenue onto the drive that led behind Hayford's office. He parked in back and bounded up the stairs to the back door. Blake Nicholas was waiting for him as he entered the war room.

Castille tossed the envelope on a table. Nicholas looked up at him.

"That's it?"

"That's it. Phone records from the church for the past two years. That should bracket us around the dates we're working with." Castille pulled up a chair. "You need to go through all of this. Enter it in the computer as you go, but make sure you pay attention. Sometimes those programs aren't as much help as a sharp eye."

"Okay." Nicholas opened the envelope and slid out a stack of papers about an inch thick. "Too bad they couldn't just e-mail all this to us."

Castille shook his head.

"No way. All that stuff would go through their internal network. Somebody would see it and start asking questions about where all that account information was going."

Nicholas turned to a computer and punched several keys. A program appeared on the monitor. He began entering information.

Twenty-one

A few minutes later Scott returned to the courtroom with Collins by his side. As they walked up the aisle, the bailiff disappeared through a door behind the judge's bench. Soon Judge McKenzie appeared.

"All right, gentlemen. Are we ready to resume?"

Somerset stood.

"Yes, Your Honor. I think so."

"Very well." She turned to Scott. "Rev. Nolan."

Scott returned to the witness stand. He looked over at Somerset.

"Would you repeat your question?"

Somerset turned to the court reporter.

"Could you read that back to him, please?"

The court reporter read from the transcript.

"What topics did you talk about?"

Scott hesitated, then replied.

"We talked about his work. His family. His wife."

"Did he tell you anything that indicated something might be amiss in his life? Did the nature of that conversation lead you to believe something was wrong?"

"Yes."

For a moment Scott could see Attaway, a cigar in his mouth, hands wrapped around a fishing rod, the relaxed, easy look he had when there was nothing to do but fish. Then, just as quickly, the image vanished and there was Somerset and the stark reality of the courtroom.

Somerset cut his eye at the judge. She leaned down from her bench.

"Rev. Nolan."

Inside himself, Scott felt like he was violating the trust of a friend. Still, faced with the option of either answering or going to jail, he answered.

"He was distant. He wasn't as outgoing as he'd been. Not as talkative. He usually had something to say about everything. But that day he was brooding."

"Had you ever seen him like this before?"

"He'd been like that when I saw him earlier in the week."

"When was the next time you saw him before that Saturday when you went fishing? Working backwards. Before that Saturday. When did you see him?"

"Thursday afternoon. He came by the office after lunch. Said he was going fishing that Saturday. Wanted to know if I wanted to come with him."

"And you noticed something was wrong?"

"Yes."

"Did you ask him about it then?"

"No."

"Did he tell you something was wrong?"

"No."

"Did he suggest to you that he wanted you to go fishing with him because he had something he wanted to talk about?"

"No."

"You just thought he seemed a little different."

"He was not himself."

"Now while you were out there that Saturday fishing. Did he talk about what was bothering him?"

"He tried to. I think he wanted to. But then he just stopped. Wouldn't say anything about it."

"What did he say? In the little that he did say."

"For most of the trip he wasn't really talking about anything. I tried to get him to talk about fishing. Asked about his family. His children. Just trying to get him to talk. Fishing. Boats. Women. Anything. Finally got him to talk a little about football. He was a big Alabama fan. They'd beaten up Ole Miss the year before. I'm an Ole Miss graduate. We talked about that awhile." Scott felt a lump in his throat. He swallowed hard and kept talking. "Then I just asked him what was wrong. He said, 'There are people I do business with who have me ...' And then he stopped. I tried to get him to tell me about it. He just shook his head. I can see him right now. He shook his head. Looked at me with a big, wide grin. And said, 'Preach, I'd love to tell you, but it's better for your family if you don't know.'"

"That's all he said, 'It's better for your family if you don't know'?"

"Yes."

"How did you come to know Mr. Attaway?"

"He was one of our members."

"Do you recall the first time you met him?"

"We met at a wedding. Not long after I came to St. Pachomius, I conducted a wedding for his niece. He and I met at the rehearsal."

Judge McKenzie interrupted.

"Is this Keyton Attaway the lawyer we're talking about?"

Somerset nodded.

"Yes, Your Honor."

"And he was murdered a couple of years ago?"

"Yes, Your Honor."

"Mr. Somerset, how is this conversation relevant to your defense of this lawsuit?"

"I prefer not to instruct the witness about what I'm looking for."

"I can't rule on your motion unless you tell me why you want this information."

Somerset stood there for a moment, a pained look on his face. Finally, his shoulders slumped and he responded.

"If this case goes to trial, we expect one of the key witnesses at that trial will be Mike Connolly. But because Mr. Connolly is a lawyer, there are things about his affairs that he can't tell us or won't tell us. Things that are clearly privileged matters. I'm trying to get at some of that through other witnesses. Rev. Nolan is one of those witnesses. I think I'm entitled to find out all I can about Mr. Connolly, generally and specifically. Rev. Nolan was associated with him on matters involved in this lawsuit and on other matters. The rules of procedure allow me to depose him on matters that are evidentiary as to this lawsuit and on matters that might lead to admissible evidence in this lawsuit. That's all I'm trying to do."

Judge McKenzie nodded thoughtfully.

"You're entitled to depose him on matters that might reasonably lead to admissible evidence."

"Asking this witness about Mr. Connolly's cases fits within the scope of questions allowed by the rules."

"Anything else?"

"No, Your Honor."

Judge McKenzie looked around the room.

"Anyone else have anything for this witness?"

There was no response. She looked at Collins.

"Mr. Collins, you want to ask your client anything on the record?"

Collins stood.

"Yes, Your Honor."

"Very well."

Collins crossed the room and stood in front of Scott.

"Rev. Nolan, was Keyton Attaway one of your parishioners?"

"Yes."

"A member of your church."

"Yes."

"Came to see you about many things."

"Yes."

"Sought spiritual guidance from you."

"Yes."

"Comfort."

"Yes."

"Advice."

"Yes."

"When he wanted to talk with you about these things, did he always come to the church?"

"No."

"Where did he talk to you about these things?"

"His house. My house. While we were fishing. His beach house. Over lunch."

"Numerous places."

"Yes."

"In fact, did you ever discuss these matters with him in a formal counseling setting? In your office."

"Only once."

Collins glanced up at Judge McKenzie.

"Nothing further, Your Honor."

"Very well." Judge McKenzie looked over at Somerset. "Anything further from you, Mr. Somerset?"

Somerset stood.

"We would argue, Your Honor, that while Mr. Attaway may have sought Rev. Nolan's help in various settings, the nature of this particular conversation the Saturday before his murder was not of a pastoral or confessional nature and not protected by the priest-penitent privilege."

Judge McKenzie nodded.

"Mr. Collins."

Collins stood.

"We contend that it was. As Rev. Nolan has testified, his relationship with Mr. Attaway was such that they had many pastoral conversations in a variety of settings, and we would argue the conversation in question is protected by the privilege."

Judge McKenzie stood.

"Very well. Give me a minute, gentlemen."

Twenty-two

*A*fter a late start Glover finally reached an exit from the interstate for Marianna, Florida. Getting there had taken four hours. It seemed like four days. He steered the car onto the exit ramp and followed the highway signs toward town.

Small and quaint, the town was built around a central courthouse square. Two business streets ran parallel to the square. Glover made a lap around the square and cruised both streets. Within five minutes he'd seen the entire town.

The receipt Castille had located from Scott Nolan's credit card account came from Jordan's Chevron, a gas station on the highway between town and the interstate. Glover had passed it earlier. He made one more lap around the courthouse square and then drove back to the station.

A rusted blue and white sign hung from a pole near the road. Beneath it were three gas pumps perched atop a concrete island. Around the pumps was a gravel parking lot stained brown from years of oil and grime.

The station building looked like something from a bygone era, with curves instead of corners and glass blocks around the doors and windows. Worn-out tires were piled to one side. Three cars sat along a fence that separated the station from an open field.

Glover parked near the building and went inside.

A man wearing gray shorts and a gray uniform shirt came from the service bay. His head was shaved, and he had on a pair of canvas shoes held together with duct tape wrapped around the toes. He smiled at Glover as he came near.

"Afternoon."

Glover nodded.

"Good afternoon."

"Something I can help you with?"

Glover took a copy of the receipt from his pocket and held it for the man to see.

"A guy named Scott Nolan bought some gas from you sometime last year. Does that name mean anything to you?"

The man took the receipt and held it at arm's length.

"Scott Nolan?"

Glover nodded.

"Yes. Recognize the name?"

The man stared at the receipt a moment, then shook his head.

"No. Can't say that I do."

He handed the receipt to Glover and folded his arms across his chest. Glover sighed.

"I didn't think so. You probably get quite a few customers in here."

The man grinned.

"Yeah. Some days." He looked around. "Some days not near enough."

Glover took a picture of Scott Nolan from his pocket.

"This is what he looked like."

The man glanced at the photograph and shook his head.

"I don't think I've ever seen him. Sorry. Something wrong with the transaction?"

Glover shook his head.

"Not really." He took another photograph from his pocket. "This woman might have been traveling with him. Do you recognize her?"

The man ran his hand over the top of his head as he stared at the picture.

"No. Can't say that I do." He grinned. "She's pretty. But she doesn't look like she's from around here."

"She's not."

The man pointed to the picture.

"Looks like someone from the Middle East."

Glover glanced around.

"Actually she's from Bosnia."

The man looked perplexed.

"Bosnia?"

Glover nodded. The man repeated himself.

"Bosnia." He looked at Glover. "That's one of those countries Clinton sent all those troops to, ain't it?"

Glover smiled.

"Yes. It is. I think some of them are still there." Glover returned the photograph to his pocket. "Listen, is there a hotel around here where they might have stayed?"

The man's face turned serious.

"Only hotel around here is on the other road from the interstate."

Glover frowned.

"The other road?"

The man nodded.

"There's two exits that lead into town. This one and one about three miles west. Which way'd you come?"

"Interstate."

"From Tallahassee?"

Glover hesitated, then lied.

"Yeah."

"Well, if you get back on the interstate and go west a little farther. Like you was going to Pensacola. You'll come to another Marianna exit. It's not far. Just down the highway a little ways. Get off there and the hotel is up there on the left."

"Okay." Glover brushed his hands together. "What's the name of it?"

The man chuckled.

"Marianna Motel."

Twenty-three

*T*hirty minutes later Judge McKenzie entered the courtroom and took a seat at the bench.

"All right. I'm ready. Everyone here?"

Somerset nodded. Judge McKenzie began.

"The priest-penitent privilege protects a broader range of priest-parishioner interaction than merely that of hearing a confession. It covers all those conversations in which a parishioner at an established church seeks the spiritual counsel and comfort of a licensed, ordained minister. I assume Rev. Nolan and his church fit that category. Anyone here contest that?"

There was no response. Judge McKenzie continued.

"The privilege is designed to protect both parties—priest and parishioner—and all parties present at the time of the conversation at issue. The privilege is to be construed in a liberal fashion so long as it meets the test of being for the purpose of spiritual aid, counsel, and comfort.

"The conversation before us today was not a conversation which Mr. Attaway initiated. It was one initiated by Rev. Nolan. Clearly, topics such as who won the latest ball game or the general banter men often have about women would not fit within that privilege. Nor would disclosures made to a priest by a parishioner that indicated the parishioner was about to commit a crime.

"In this instance Mr. Attaway appears to have responded to Rev. Nolan's questions in a cautious manner. In a manner which could be construed as indicating he did not consider the conversation privileged. Mr. Attaway was an attorney, and we could assume he was aware a privilege of this nature existed. Telling Rev. Nolan that it would be better for his family if Rev. Nolan didn't know the answer to the questions tells me Mr. Attaway thought that others would learn the content of his answer. Inasmuch as Mr. Attaway and Rev. Nolan were the only people present, the only way that could happen would be for Rev. Nolan to tell. If Mr. Attaway thought the nature of the conversation was such that Rev. Nolan could talk about it, or would feel free to talk about it, and very well might talk about what he would say, then I don't think we're under any constraint to think the conversation was privileged.

"So I find the conversation was not a conversation protected by the priest-penitent privilege. The deponent will answer counsel's questions."

Judge McKenzie glanced around the room one last time.

"Court is adjourned."

As she rose from the bench, everyone in the room stood.

Twenty-four

*T*hat night Hayford met Braxton for dinner at the Lighthouse Restaurant in Bayou La Batre. They sat at a table in the corner and talked while they ate.

Hayford scooped up a spoonful of gumbo.

"Haven't seen you around much lately."

Braxton took a drink of iced tea.

"Busy."

"What's her name?"

Braxton grinned.

"You wouldn't know her."

"I don't want to know her."

Hayford wiped his mouth on a napkin. Over Braxton's shoulder he saw a man standing in the doorway.

"Do you know the man who's standing up there near the door?"

Braxton looked puzzled.

"Do what?"

"Don't make a big deal of it. There's a man standing back there by the door. Do you know him?"

Braxton took another sip of tea and glanced over his shoulder.

"That's Cootie Stork."

Hayford's face twisted in a disbelieving look.

"Cootie?"

"Yeah."

"How do you know him?"

"I don't really know him. I just know who he is. Everybody knows Cootie."

"He's been looking this way for a long time. I just wondered if you knew him."

Braxton smiled.

"A little jumpy, aren't you?"

"I wish we could get this thing over with."

"What happened today?"

"Judge told the priest to answer Somerset's questions or go to jail."

Braxton wiped his mouth on the napkin.

"That should move things along."

"Maybe."

"What was he asking about?"

Hayford cut his eyes at Braxton. Braxton frowned.

"What?"

"Keyton Attaway."

Braxton leaned away from the table.

"That's not good. Why's he asking about that?"

Hayford shrugged.

"Thinks he has to get into it. I mean, we told him to ask about Mike Connolly, so you knew this had to come up."

"What's he said about him?"

"Nothing yet."

"What's he know?"

"The priest?"

"Yeah."

Hayford shrugged.

"How would I know?"

Braxton gave him a sarcastic smile.

"Yeah, right. You don't know anything." He leaned forward and took a bite. "Think any of it will hurt us?"

"Won't hurt me. I never dealt with Attaway."

"No. You had me do it for you."

Hayford smiled.

"Relax. The priest won't know anything that touches us. And even if he did, no one in the room except me will understand what he's talking about."

"Where's Glover?"

"On an errand."

"Doing any good?"

Hayford took a bite of fish.

"Haven't heard yet."

Braxton reached for the hot sauce.

"He never called me anymore after we went to that convenience store."

"He wasn't impressed by your performance."

"Any other places we could look?"

Hayford gestured with the spoon in his hand.

"He already found it."

Braxton looked surprised.

"He found a photograph of her?"

"Yeah."

"Where'd he get it?"

"The condo."

Braxton's eyes were wide.

"You told him about the condo?"

"Just the location."

"Was I in the picture?"

"Not in the one he gave me."

Twenty-five

hree days later Scott was back in Somerset's office, seated at the end of the conference table. Somerset and Hayford sat to his left. Jessica Stabler and Sarah sat to the right. Around them was a sea of lawyers.

Somerset glanced at the court reporter, then turned to Scott.

"I believe we were talking about your fishing trips with Keyton Attaway. What did you talk about while you were out there fishing? On that last fishing trip."

"Not much. He was rather distant."

"Earlier you said he appeared upset. What about him made you think he was upset?"

"I don't know if *upset* is the right word. He just wasn't himself. Wasn't as outgoing as he'd been. Not as talkative. He usually had something to say about everything. But that day he was in a funk. Brooding. He'd been like that when I saw him earlier in the week."

"When did you see him before that Saturday when you went fishing?"

"Thursday afternoon. He came by the office after lunch. Said he was going fishing that Saturday. Asked if I wanted to come with him."

"Is that all he talked about that day? That Thursday?"

"Yes."

"Did he talk about what was bothering him?"

"Like I said in court, he tried once or twice that Saturday. I think he wanted to. But then he just stopped. Wouldn't say anything about it."

"Now you said you came to know Mr. Attaway at a wedding reception."

"Rehearsal."

"What wedding was that?"

"His niece. Jenny Sessions."

"That's her married name? Sessions?"

"No. She married a guy named Kirkwood. Kevin Kirkwood."

"Did you see Keyton Attaway on other occasions after that, other than at church?"

"Yes."

"What were those occasions?"

"Not long after I met him, we had a legal problem or two at the church. Since I knew he was a lawyer, I called him about it. We talked. I think I went to his office a couple of times. Got to talking about various things. He had a boat. Found out I enjoyed fishing. He invited me to go fishing with him."

"So you went fishing."

"Yes."

"How many different times did you go fishing with Mr. Attaway?"

"Hard to say."

"Best guess."

"Maybe a dozen times a year. I don't know."

"A year?"

"Yes."

"Where did you put in?"

"The boat was tied up at a marina on Dauphin Island."

"This was a big boat?"

"Thirty-five feet."

"How far out did you go?"

"I don't know. Way out past the edge."

"The edge?"

"Where the water drops off. Gets really deep."

"Gone all day?"

"Usually."

"What did you do out there? Not that Saturday, but just generally."

"Fished. Smoked cigars. Drank a few beers."

Whispers went around the room. Somerset kept going.

"Drank a few beers?"

"Yes."

"You don't have a problem with that?"

"With what?"

"Smoking a cigar and drinking a beer."

"Why would I have a problem with that?"

"Your church members don't mind?"

"I don't know."

"Isn't that against the rules?"

"There's no rule against smoking a cigar and drinking a beer while you're fishing."

Someone spoke up.

"Sounds like my kind of church."

Everyone laughed. Scott smiled.

"You really should see the movie."

Somerset frowned.

"The movie?"

Goolsby spoke up.

"*The Matrix.*"

Somerset looked at Scott.

"What are you saying?"

"The world around you is a lie."

"A lie?"

"Yes. A lie. Told to keep you from knowing the truth."

"That I can go fishing and drink a few beers and smoke a cigar."

"That you don't have to feel guilty about it."

Somerset looked away.

"Now that Saturday when you were out there, drinking beer and smoking cigars, he didn't loosen up? More than that one conversation you've told us about?"

"Not really. I'm not sure we had more than two beers apiece. We never got drunk, anyway. But I don't think we had much at all that day. It was a different kind of day. Like he knew something was wrong or something was happening."

"When you were out there like that, fishing, did he ever talk to you about his clients?"

"Not by name."

"But he talked about them."

"He would sometimes mention something about a case he had. You know, not really talking about any particular person. He'd just sometimes talk about something humorous that might have happened in a trial or a deposition or something like that."

"Did he ever mention Buie Hayford?"

"No. I don't recall it if he did."

"Ever tell you anything about Tidewater National Bank?"

"I don't think so. He never mentioned anyone by name."

"Do you recall anything in particular he told you about any of his clients?"

"No."

"Did you do anything else together besides fish?"

"He and Karen came over to our house a few times. We went to theirs. Parties."

"What parties?"

"Just parties at other church members' homes. Friends. That sort of thing."

"Like what parties? Name them."

"I can't really ... Tootsie Trehern's birthday party. I think I mentioned it before. That was after he died, but he would have been at that if he'd been alive. Karen was there."

"The party you were telling us about where you met Frank Ingram?"

"Yes. He and Karen were friends with Tootsie. He would have been there."

"Ever take any trips with him? Other than the fishing trips?"

"Yes."

"Where did you go?"

"A group of men from the church went rafting on a river up in North Carolina summer before last."

Scott and Goolsby exchanged looks. Somerset seemed not to notice.

"Did you take any other trips with him?"

"The winter before Keyton died, another group wanted to go snow skiing. They took me with them."

"Where did you go on that trip? The skiing trip."

"Beaver Creek, Colorado."

"Who went on that first trip, the one to ..." Somerset paused. He scrawled a note on his legal pad, then checked his watch. "You know, let's take a break."

Twenty-six

Unable to find anything further in Marianna, Glover spent the night there at the Marianna Motel. When he awoke the next morning, he thought about returning to Mobile, but he still had cash in his pocket that Hayford had given him for the trip and nothing pressing at home. So instead of driving west, he went south. For the past year and a half, all he'd heard about was how this priest and some guy named Hollis Toombs drove a church van full of prostitutes to a beach house on Cape San Blas. With nothing better to do, Glover decided to see the place for himself.

The ride from Marianna took about an hour and a half. Glover reached the turnoff for the cape about ten thirty that morning. He rode through piney woods and sandy hills for what seemed like a long way. Finally, he began to see patches of blue water through the trees. Somewhere along the way he passed a café named Simone's. A single car was parked out front.

Two miles past the café, the road made a sharp turn to the right. He slowed the car and let it coast through the curve. The road straightened. White, sandy beach appeared on the left. He lowered the windows. Warm, humid air filled the car with the smell of salt water. The sound of waves crashing on the shore rose over the noise of the tires on the pavement. Glover slowed the car even more and stared at the beach.

A little way down he passed a single-story beach house. Built of wood, it was unpainted and weathered gray by years of scorching sunshine and blustery hurricanes. Beyond it a berm rose from the road. A driveway trail turned off the pavement and disappeared behind the sand. Craning his neck, Glover caught a glimpse of a roof as he idled past.

The next house had three stories with a screened porch on each level. It sat back from the road in a stand of pine trees. The next two houses were just like it. Glover drove all the way to the state park at the end of the pavement, then turned around and drove back to the curve.

For all of his driving and searching, Glover found nothing that looked to him like it might be the house where the women had stayed. No signs identified any of them as belonging to Rick Connolly, and the scenery brought nothing to mind from what little Hayford and the others had said about it. When he reached the curve, he pressed the gas pedal. The car picked up speed.

"Just another wild idea," he mumbled.

He raised the windows and reached for the volume control on the radio. Just then he passed the café he'd seen on the way down. Four cars were parked there now. A new idea came to his mind.

When he reached a place where the shoulder of the road was wide enough for the car, he turned around and drove back. By the time he reached the café, there were five cars in the parking lot.

Inside, a jukebox played a ten-year-old Jimmy Buffet song. Four people sat at a bar along the wall opposite the door. Glover crossed the room to an empty stool and propped his elbows on the bar. A man came from the far end.

"What could I get you?"

"What's good?"

"Everything."

"How about a hamburger. You got a good hamburger?"

"Best one on the cape."

The man next to Glover chuckled and leaned over to him.

"It's the only one on the cape."

Glover smiled.

"Medium well. Everything but onions."

The man behind the bar wiped his hands on a dirty towel.

"What you drinking?"

On the wall across from Glover was a Heineken sign.

"Heineken."

A cooler sat behind the bar. The man slid back the lid, took out a bottle of beer, and twisted off the cap. He laid a paper napkin on the bar and set the bottle on it, then moved away.

Glover took a sip. The man next to him looked over at him.

"You come down for a few days?"

Glover shook his head.

"Just looking around."

"Where you from?"

"Mobile."

"I been to Mobile once. Mardi Gras. Once was enough."

"Yeah. You gotta be in the right mood for Mardi Gras." Glover took another sip from the bottle. "Listen, I was looking for a house down here. Owned by a guy in Birmingham named Rick Connolly. Ever hear of him? Know where his house might be?"

The man shook his head.

"Name doesn't sound familiar." He leaned over to the man beside him.

"You ever hear of a place down here owned by some guy named Rick Connolly?"

The second man shrugged. Glover leaned around to see him.

"A doctor. In Birmingham."

The man shook his head.

"Friend of yours?"

"Sort of."

He took the photograph of Tatiana from his pocket.

"About a year and a half ago, he had some women staying at his place."

Everyone at the bar smiled and nodded. Glover held the picture so they could see.

"This woman was one of the ones who was there."

Someone down the bar chimed in.

"How many were there?"

Glover raised himself up to see who spoke. An older man near the end of the bar caught his eye.

"I remember a bunch of women at the house next to me," the man said.

"This would have been about a dozen."

The man nodded.

"That's about right. Foreign women. Couldn't speak a word of English."

Glover's eyes grew wide.

"That's them. You know where that place is?"

The man slipped off his stool and came down the bar.

"If you go down here around the curve, couple of houses down you'll see a sign that says On Call. That's it. That's the one you're looking for."

"On Call?"

"Yeah. I think the guy must be a doctor or something. Never anybody down there much."

The man stepped away. Glover's hamburger arrived. He took a sip of beer and began to eat.

Twenty-seven

Scott came from the hallway with a cup of coffee. He picked up a doughnut from the table by the door and squeezed through the crowded room to the chair at the end of the table.

Somerset was already seated. He waited until Scott was in the chair, then started.

"Who went—"

Someone spoke up.

"Everyone isn't back yet."

Somerset looked down the table.

"If they want to spend the morning returning calls and drinking coffee, that's their business. I'm not waiting on them."

Somerset turned back to Scott.

"When we took a break we were talking about some trips. Two trips. One to North Carolina and another to Colorado. Who went on the first trip? The one to North Carolina."

"I don't remember exactly. Keyton was there. Bob Dorsey. Jon Morgan. A couple more. I can't remember their names right now."

"These are all members of your church?"

"Yes."

"What about the second trip? The one to Colorado."

"Mike Maitre, David Webster. Some of the same guys that were on the rafting trip. Claude Warren."

"Was Keyton Attaway friends with any of these men you've mentioned from either of these two trips?"

"He was pretty good friends with Jon Morgan. They went fishing together a few times. I'm not sure how close he was to the others."

"You have addresses for all these men?"

"Yes."

"I'd like addresses for all the men you mentioned. And the names and addresses of the others on those two trips if you have them someplace. You know, a list or whatever."

"I'll see what I have."

"Did anything happen on the rafting trip?"

"Not anything out of the ordinary. Took a rafting trip down a river. The Ocoee. Had a good steak in Cashiers."

"How many days were you up there?"

"Three or four. I think the rafting part took all of one day."

"Anything else happen while you were on that trip?"

"Nothing extraordinary."

"Was Keyton Attaway there with the group the entire time?"

"Yes."

"You saw him—"

Scott interrupted.

"No."

Somerset looked perplexed.

"Excuse me?"

"There was one day. He left the group for a few hours. Said he had to meet someone and take care of some business."

"Did he say who that someone was?"

"No."

"How did he get away? How did he go?" Somerset held up his hand. "Wait a minute. Don't answer that." He took a breath. "Let's back up. Where were you staying?"

"We were at the Highfield Inn. It's a lodge up in the mountains."

"So you weren't roughing it."

"No."

"Plenty of beer and cigars."

"They don't allow smoking in the buildings or the rooms. If you want to smoke a cigar you have to walk out on one of the trails."

"Lots to do there?"

"Not too much. Horseback riding. Swimming. The river. Hiking."

"How did you get up there?"

"We drove."

"Did Attaway drive?"

"Yes."

"So when he slipped away that day, he drove himself?"

"No. He and I rode up there together. When he left that day, the day he slipped away for a while, he gave me the keys. Said he wasn't sure when he'd get back. If I needed to go somewhere, I could use his car."

"So how did he leave?"

"Someone picked him up."

"Who was it? Did you see them?"

"I don't know who it was."

"What did you see?"

"Right after breakfast a black Suburban pulled up in front of the main building. Keyton went out. Somebody got out of the Suburban, opened the door for him. Keyton got in. They drove away."

"Get a look at the person who opened the door?"

"Not really."

"Anyone else in the Suburban? Was this person the driver?"

"I'm not sure."

"You couldn't see inside it?"

"Not very well. The windows were tinted."

"Do you think, based on what you saw that day, there was someone else in the Suburban, other than the person who opened the door and, perhaps, a driver?"

"I don't know."

"Notice anything else about Keyton Attaway that morning?"

Scott remembered the moment Keyton ducked his head to get in the Suburban. He nodded thoughtfully.

"All the laughter left him."

"The laughter left him?"

"Yes."

Goolsby interrupted.

"Back in the matrix."

Scott raised an eyebrow.

"Exactly. He was back in the matrix."

Somerset sighed.

"I need to see that movie."

Scott's face brightened.

"Yes, you do."

"What does that mean? 'Back in the matrix'?"

"You'd have to see the movie to understand. Or talk to that man down there." Scott glanced down the table at Goolsby. "I think he's seen it."

Goolsby smiled. Scott continued.

"It was like ... He'd been free. But now he had to go back to a world of slavery. Not going back as a freeman, but to engage it as a slave. It was sad to watch him."

Somerset scribbled a note on his legal pad.

"Do you think you would recognize the man who opened the door for him as he was getting in the Suburban?"

"Probably."

"What did he look like?"

"Tall. Athletic. He was in shape. He looked fit. Short haircut. Dark sunglasses. Gray suit. White shirt. Red tie. Had a pin on his lapel."

"You just described a room full of lawyers."

"Yes, except for the sunglasses."

"Now, Mr. Attaway left in this black Suburban. Did he ... Did you see the tag on the Suburban as it left?"

"No. They drove off. I went back inside."

"So Keyton Attaway left the lodge where you all were staying. Anyone else see him go?"

"I don't know."

"No one else was out there as he was leaving?"

"David came along about the time I went back inside. He might have seen something."

"David?"

"Webster. David Webster."

"He was on this trip? I thought he was on the trip to Colorado."

"He was. He was on both trips."

"What does Mr. Webster do? Where does he work?"

"He works for a drilling company."

"He lives here? In Mobile?"

"Not now. I think he took a job in Texas or someplace. Somebody said the other day he was over in Iraq, I think. I don't know. He was from Texas."

"Okay. Now, Attaway left the lodge. But he returned."

"Yes."

"When did he return?"

"He left sometime after breakfast. He got back right before dinner."

"So he was gone all day."

"Yes."

"Anyone ask about him? Other than David Webster?"

"I think Mike Maitre asked where he was."

"Maitre was on this trip too?"

"Yes."

"And what did you tell him? What did you tell Mr. Maitre?"

"I told him something came up that he had to go see about. Something like that."

"When he came back ... When Attaway came back to the lodge, did you and he talk about where he'd been?"

"Not really. I asked him if everything was all right. He said yes. Then we had dinner."

"See him anymore that night?"

"Yes. We were in the same room."

"The two of you roomed together?"

"Yes."

"Anyone else stay in that room with you?"

"No."

"Did you talk later that night?"

"About where he'd been?"

"Yes."

"No."

"Talk about anything else that night?"

"I'm sure we did, but I can't remember any of the details."

"See anything, hear anything, find anything that made you wonder what he'd been doing?"

"Not really."

"When you say 'not really,' my interest level goes way up. What did you see or hear or find that made you curious?"

"Well ... that night, after dinner and after everything else, we were back in the room. I wanted to look at a book I'd brought, but it was in Keyton's car. The car keys and his wallet were lying on the dresser. So I reached over there to get them. There was this thing that looked like the remote entry for the car doors. When I picked it up, he snapped at me. Told me to leave it alone."

"Told you to leave the remote to the car alone?"

"It wasn't the remote. I thought it was the remote. He didn't say what it was. He just picked up the keys and handed them to me. The remote for the car was on the key ring."

"What did this other thing look like? The thing he didn't want you to touch."

"Little square thing about that big."

Somerset glanced over at the court reporter.

"The reporter needs a verbal description."

"Excuse me?"

Somerset pointed.

"She needs a verbal answer."

"Oh. Yeah. Sorry. It was a black device about an inch long. Less than an inch wide. There was a small button in the center. It had a ring attached to one end like you'd slip on a key ring."

"Have you ever seen anything like it, anything similar?"

"Just the remote entry thing for my own car."

"Those usually have more than one button. One for the doors. One for the horn. Maybe one for the alarm. This one only had one button?"

"Yes. After he snapped at me, I realized it probably wasn't what I thought it was."

"Did he give you any explanation for what it might be or for his reaction?"

"No. No explanation. He said something like 'Sorry. Didn't mean to snap.' Something like that."

"How was he? When he returned. Was he upset?"

"No. I don't think so. I mean, I don't remember thinking that about him at the time."

"But he snapped at you."

"Yes. But I didn't think he was in a bad mood or anything. That wasn't my impression. I just reached for something he didn't want me to get and he reacted."

"Did you go to the car that night?"

"The car?"

"For the book. You said you were going to the car for a book. Did you?"

"Yes."

"See anything in the car that night that made you suspicious or curious? Anything out of the ordinary."

"No."

"Anything else unusual happen on that trip?"

"No."

"Okay. Now the trip to Colorado. Who was on that trip?"

"Pretty much the same people."

"Keyton Attaway. You. Mike Maitre. David Webster. Bob Dorsey."

"I don't think Bob went on that trip."

"Bob Dorsey?"

"Yeah. I don't think he went with us to Colorado."

"Okay. Anyone else on that trip?"

"There were some more. Claude Warren. David's brother-in-law was there. Some others, but I can't remember them right now."

"And you went to Beaver Creek?"

"Yes."

"Rather expensive place."

"Yes. It was."

"Being a priest must pay well."

Scott did not reply. Somerset pressed the point.

"You paid for your own trip?"

"No."

"Who paid?"

"I'm not going to tell you."

Larry King sighed and leaned away from the table. Scott continued.

"It wasn't Keyton Attaway, and it has nothing to do with this case, and I'm not telling you."

"Why not?"

"Because it's none of your business."

Twenty-eight

*I*t was twelve thirty when the deposition broke for lunch. Hayford left Somerset's office and took the elevator to the lobby. He walked from the building up the street to his car and slipped in behind the steering wheel. As he glanced in the mirror to check for traffic, he saw a man sitting in the rear seat.

A smile crept across Hayford's face.

"Hello, Tony."

Tony nodded.

"I thought we should talk."

Hayford looked indifferent.

"Sure. Where'd you have in mind?"

Tony gave a backhanded wave.

"Drive."

Hayford steered the car away from the curb and started up the street. At the corner he turned right onto Dauphin Street and drove away from town.

Past Broad Street, Hayford caught Tony's eye in the mirror.

"You just get into town?"

"Never mind about that. Everybody wants to know what's happening with this case."

"The lawsuit?"

"Yeah."

Hayford dismissed the question with a shrug.

"That's nothing."

"Everybody's a little worried. You know. They think this thing may not work out right."

"What's not to work out?"

"Lawyers."

"Lawyers?"

"They get to asking questions, they sometimes get into things that should be left alone."

"Nah." Hayford shook his head. "It's nothing to worry about. Besides, if they win, the insurance will pay most of it."

Tony's face lost all expression.

"Nobody's worried about the money."

"So what are they worried about? The lawyers ask a few questions. That's what they do. No one knows anything, and even if they do, no one in the room knows what they're talking about."

"They're worried about that old lady."

Hayford lifted his hand from the steering wheel in a dismissive gesture.

"Come on, she's just an old lady. A grandmother."

"Yeah, well, they're worried about her. And when they worry, I worry."

"What they ought to be worried about is that grand jury."

Tony turned away.

"That grand jury is your problem. You messed that up. You get to fix it."

Hayford didn't like the tone of his voice. He avoided the mirror and drove in silence. Tony shifted his position on the seat.

"What's the matter, you lose interest in our conversation?"

"I'm working on it. Okay?"

"I hear you aren't making much progress."

"Hey, we found a photograph of her. I have people out there, beating the bushes."

"That's not what they need to beat."

"Listen, I got a guy in Florida running things down. He's getting close."

Tony scoffed.

"John Glover couldn't find his way home." He leaned over the seat and pointed. "Pull over up here."

To the right a Cadillac was parked at the curb. Hayford pulled in behind it. Tony patted him on the shoulder.

"We gotta stop meeting like this. People will talk."

He opened the door and stepped out.

Twenty-nine

When Glover finished eating the hamburger at Simone's, he drove back to the curve and down the shoreline. As he approached the fourth house, he saw a white sign with faded blue letters.

On Call.

Glover turned the car from the pavement onto a sandy, well-worn trail that wound beneath tall pine trees to a three-story house. Painted white, it had a porch at every level that ran all the way around. In the yard a wooden swing hung from a vine-covered frame. Not far away a rusted grill sat beneath a pine tree. Glover brought the car to a stop near the swing and got out.

A breeze whispered through the tops of the pines as he made his way to the front steps. He pushed open the screen door and stepped onto the porch. His footsteps echoed against the wooden floor. The top half of the front door had a large window. He cupped his hands around his eyes and peered inside.

Directly opposite the door, a wide hallway ran through the center of the house. To the left was a large, open room that took up half of the first floor. A doorway to the right led from the hall to a dining room. Glover could see the corner of the dining table. Beyond it was a door to the kitchen. A sink in the kitchen sat beneath a window that looked out on the backyard. He could see all the way through the window to a clothesline out back.

Glover tried the door knob. To his surprise it was unlocked. He pushed open the door and went inside.

In the room to the left he made his way around a sofa and coffee table covered with magazines. He checked the dates. Most of the magazines were three years old. Along the wall was a built-in bookcase painted pale green. A television sat on the middle shelf.

Next to it lay a stack of DVDs.

Glover picked up a DVD and checked the title. As he put it back, his eye fell on a small, round dish farther down the shelf. In the dish was a business card. He picked it up and read it aloud. "Janet Freeland. State Department." Glover chewed on his bottom lip. "Why would there be a card from someone at the ..."

Without thinking, he turned the card over. On the back was a telephone number written in blue ink. He took the cell phone from his pocket and punched in the number. When he pressed the key to send the call, he heard a rapidly beeping busy signal. He checked the phone. A message on the screen indicated there was no service. He closed the phone and shoved it in his pocket.

Thirty

*T*atiana stared at the Styrofoam box and picked through the food with a plastic fork. After a few bites she tossed the fork aside and took a sip of Coca-Cola. Gina glanced over at her.

"You're not eating."

"I can't stand this place."

"It keeps you alive."

"But it takes the life from me."

Gina smiled. Tatiana glared at her.

"What are you smiling at me for?" She threw her hands in the air. "You get to go home to your family. This is just a job for you. Me, I have to live like this every day and every night."

Gina grinned.

"You want to go for a walk?"

"Yes. I would love to go for a walk. I've been telling you that for weeks. I'm stuck in here like some animal." She sighed and folded her arms across her chest. "If I'd known it would be like this I would have kept my mouth shut."

Gina was still grinning.

"I'm asking you if you want to go for a walk."

Tatiana looked away.

"We both know that isn't going to happen."

Gina rose from the table and disappeared into the kitchen. Moments later she returned carrying a plastic bag. She tossed the bag on the table.

"Put this on."

Tatiana looked up at her. Gina pointed to the bag.

"Put it on. They'll be here in five minutes."

Tatiana opened the bag. Inside she found an orange baseball

cap with a green alligator stitched across the front. She gave Gina a puzzled look.

"What is this?"

"A Florida Gators hat. Help you blend into the crowd." She pointed to the sack once again. "Take the rest of it out and put it on."

Tatiana took out a pair of sunglasses and a blonde wig.

Just then there was a knock at the door. Gina pulled her pistol from the holster.

"Take that stuff into the bedroom and put it on."

Tatiana rose from the table. When she was out of sight down the hall, Gina opened the door.

Thirty-one

Scott returned early from lunch. He wasn't very hungry and he had nowhere else to go. He took a seat at the conference table and waited. In a few minutes the lawyers filed back into the room. Before long, Somerset arrived, followed by Hayford. When they were seated, Somerset glanced at his notes from the morning and began.

"We were talking about this trip you took with some of the men from your church. The trip to Beaver Creek. Where did you stay?"

"In a condo. I don't know who owned it. Just a rental."

"Who set up the trip?"

"David Webster."

"And Mr. Attaway was there?"

"Yes."

"Anything unusual happen? Mr. Attaway slip off for the day? Unusual phone call? Visitor?"

"No. It was just a ski trip. I mean that's all I knew about it. Everyone left the condo by eight. Got back around sunset. Went to dinner. I think we watched a movie one night. Most nights, everyone was too tired to move."

"Did you ski with Mr. Attaway?"

"No. That was my one and only ski trip. I spent every day in ski school."

"Mr. Attaway skied with the others?"

"Yes."

"All right. Now did you and Keyton Attaway do anything else together? Trip to North Carolina. Trip to Colorado. Fishing. Anything else?"

"I can't remember anything else. We'd stop for lunch or dinner on the way home from Dauphin Island sometimes."

"Where did you stop?"

"Bailey's. Nan-Sea. The marina at Fowl River."

"Anything out of the ordinary happen on any of those occasions?"

"No. Not that I recall. Just two fishermen coming home from a fishing trip."

"See anyone while you were at any of those places? Anyone drop by the table, that sort of thing?"

"No."

"You mentioned there was a cross in Mr. Attaway's office that you gave him. What kind of cross was it?"

"It's called the Cross of St. Anthony."

"What does it look like?"

"The cross piece goes along the top, rather than a little way down the vertical piece. Looks like a capital T."

"Why? Why did you give him that cross?"

"He reached a point about a year before he died. A turning point. A tipping point. Things had built up that were pushing him toward change. And he made the change. I gave him that cross as a reminder."

"This wasn't something that would fit in your pocket."

"No. About this high. Twelve inches. Maybe eighteen."

"A change. What kind of change? What was pushing him?"

"He'd had a few marital difficulties. His children were getting a little rambunctious. That sort of thing."

"Infidelity?"

"I wouldn't tell you about that even if I knew."

Thirty-two

Tatiana emerged from the bedroom wearing the blonde wig with the baseball cap and dark sunglasses. Four men were waiting near the door. Gina came from across the room.

"Looks like it fits."

Tatiana frowned. Gina gestured toward the men.

"These are agents from the local office. They are going with us. You might not see them while we're out, but they'll be there if something happens. I will walk beside you. While we are on the sidewalk, keep me on the outside, between you and the street. Do you understand?"

"Yes."

Gina continued.

"If we enter a store, stay within sight of me and don't wander off."

Tatiana nodded. Gina looked her in the eye.

"This is serious, Tatiana. You cannot wander away. If you get out of my sight, the agents with us will shut the place down. There'll be a big scene. We'll have to relocate you."

Tatiana sighed.

"I understand."

Gina smiled.

"Good, then." She gestured toward the door. "Let's go."

An agent opened the door. Another stepped into the corridor, checked in both directions, then motioned for them to follow. Gina guided Tatiana through the doorway and down the hall.

"Walk at a normal pace. Feel free to look around, but do not make eye contact with anyone." She caught Tatiana's eye. "You understand?"

Tatiana nodded and reached for the sunglasses.

"These are too dark for inside."

Gina grabbed her wrist.

"Don't. You must wear them at all times. Even if we're in a store."

"But I can't see."

Gina stopped.

"Tatiana, I'm sorry this isn't like a normal walk. I'm sorry life has come to this for you. Your life is never going to be like the life you imagined as a little girl. Never. But with a little effort on all our parts, you might be able to enjoy it." She took Tatiana by the elbow and nudged her forward. "Let's go."

Thirty-three

As the deposition droned on beneath him, Castille listened from the room above and worked the telephones. They'd tried to reach Glover since morning but had been unable to find him. Finally, late that afternoon, he answered his phone.

Castille was indignant.

"Where have you been?"

"Working."

"Where are you?"

"Right now I'm passing through Woodville."

Castille snapped at him.

"Don't mess with me."

"I'm not."

"Hayford's been all over me to find you. You should call in once in a while."

"I tried, but there isn't very good service out here. This is the first time the phone's worked all day."

"Where are you?"

"Woodville. I told you. Woodville." He paused for a moment. "Well, now I'm past it."

Castille reached for a map.

"Where's that located?"

"South of Tallahassee."

"What are you doing there?"

"Working my way back to the interstate."

Castille found Woodville on the map.

"What did you find in Marianna?"

"Nothing. That guy doesn't know anything."

"So what are you doing down there?"

"When I didn't find anything there, I went down to Cape San Blas."

"Anything there?"

"Not really."

"They didn't recognize her from the photograph?"

"No. They remembered the women were there, but they didn't recognize her."

"Did you find the house?"

"Yeah. I found a—"

Castille cut him off.

"Well, look, you need to go to a place called Chattahoochee." Castille traced his finger across the map. "You know where that is?"

"In Florida?"

"Yeah."

"I can find it. What's there?"

"Pull over so you can write this down. You got something to write with?"

"Yeah."

"Pull over."

"Listen, check a number for me."

"A what?"

"A number. A telephone number."

"Not now. Tell me later. Pull over. I want you to write this down."

Thirty-four

*T*atiana followed Gina down the steps to the front entrance of the apartment. They waited there while the other agents left the building. When they were gone, Gina opened the door.

"Let's go."

Tatiana followed her out the door and onto the sidewalk. The afternoon sun was bright and warm. Tatiana did her best to relish the moment. It was her first time outdoors in months.

The apartment building where Tatiana had been staying was located in a section of town popular with students at the University of Florida. Most of the people who lived there were near her own age. Many of them were from other countries. No one paid much attention to her as she walked along.

Two blocks from the apartment they turned left past a flower shop. In the middle of the block they came to Southside Market, a small store wedged between an office building and a parking deck. Tatiana paused.

"Could we get a bottle of water?"

Gina smiled.

"Sure. I could use one myself."

She guided Tatiana across the sidewalk and opened the door.

A counter ran to the right of the door, in front of the window facing the street. Behind it was a short, slender man with a balding head. Tatiana saw him as she entered. His eyes told her something was wrong.

Gina paused to let Tatiana pass, then followed her inside.

As they came around the end of the counter, Tatiana saw a young man standing in the aisle. He was about her height, dressed in sweatpants and a T-shirt. He wore a baseball cap pulled low over his eyes. In his hand was an automatic pistol. Tatiana looked away and kept walking. Behind her she heard a man's voice.

"On the floor, lady."

Tatiana hurried down the aisle toward the drink cooler at the back of the store. She heard Gina shout.

"FBI! Put the gun down!"

Tatiana peeked around the end of the shelves. Up the aisle she saw the man still standing near the cash register, the pistol in his hand.

"FBI." The man laughed. "Where's your friend? Get her up here before I shoot you both."

"You picked a bad day to rob this place. Put the gun down, and step away from the counter. I won't ask you again."

Tatiana moved to keep out of sight. Her elbow hit a jar on the shelf beside her. The jar fell to the floor and broke into pieces.

Gina shouted.

"Stop!"

Tatiana's eyes darted to the right. The man moved toward her, pointing the pistol at her and then back at Gina.

Past the next row of shelves, beyond the end of the cooler, was a door. Tatiana thought she could make it. She glanced in the man's direction once more. He pointed the pistol at her and smiled. She'd seen that kind of smile before. She knew better than to trust it.

Tatiana bolted for the door.

Thirty-five

Scott took a cup of coffee from the table near the door and moved to his chair in the conference room. Somerset waited while the other lawyers returned from the break. When everyone was in place, he began.

"So Mr. Connolly came to talk to you about Keyton Attaway. Did you talk about anything else? With Mr. Connolly."

"That first time I saw him?"

"Yes."

"He told me he had been a member of St. Pachomius previously. When Father Tagliano was there."

"I remember Father Tagliano. Used to go over there for a noon service during Lent. Nice guy."

"Yes. He was."

"Anything else? At that first meeting?"

"He told me he liked the building."

"After that first meeting with Mr. Connolly, when did you next see him?"

"I'm not sure of the exact date. He came back several times while he was working on Keyton's case. Asking questions about Keyton. I didn't know much of anything that could help him. I think he knew that. Mostly I thought he was just coming back because he liked the building."

"Did you ever know Mr. Connolly to take a drink of alcohol?"

"Yes."

"You've seen him drinking?"

"No."

"How did you know that he did?"

"I smelled it on him those first couple of times I talked with him."

"You smelled it on him? On his breath? On his clothes?"

"Yes."

"Which?"

"All of the above, I think."

"Tell us about the next visit. The next time Mike Connolly came to see you."

"One day ... This would have been several meetings after the first visit. I don't think he really came to talk about the case. As I recall, I found him sitting in the sanctuary."

"You just came through the building doing whatever you do and found him there?"

"Yes."

"What did you talk about during that visit?"

"We talked about the stained-glass windows."

"That church has some beautiful stained-glass windows."

"Yes. It does."

"You talked about them?"

"Yes."

"What about them?"

"They depict events from the life of Christ. We talked about that. He'd been to church a time or two at that point. The conversation had moved on from Keyton Attaway."

"To church. You mean on Sunday?"

"Yes."

"To St. Pachomius?"

"Yes."

"How many times? How many times had Mr. Connolly attended the Sunday service at St. Pachomius? Prior to the conversation about the stained-glass windows?"

Someone down the table spoke up.

"Who cares?"

Somerset looked frustrated.

"This is my ..." He paused a moment, then slid the cap on his pen and laid it on the table. "You know what? Let's go off the record."

Thirty-six

While everyone took a break from the deposition, Hayford slipped around the corner into the stairwell. He climbed the stairs to the next floor and entered the room where Castille sat.

"Any word from Glover?"

"I talked to him."

"Great. Where was he?"

"Florida."

"You gave him that stuff Blake found?"

"Yeah."

"Good." Hayford pulled a chair from the table and sat down. "What did you find on the priest's daughter?"

"Not much yet. We just found her yesterday."

"She's in Atlanta?"

"Yeah."

"You got anybody up there working on it?"

"Yeah."

"What about his file from that law firm?"

Castille tapped a manila folder on the table. Hayford's eyes grew wide.

"This is it?"

"Yeah."

"What's it say?"

"Don't know yet."

Hayford reached for it. Castille stopped him.

"Don't mess with it. We need it just like it is."

Hayford glared at him.

"I'm the one who signs the checks, remember?"

"I think we both know who's calling the shots on this."

Hayford leaned back.

"I don't like you talking to him behind my back."

"I know."

"But you do it anyway."

"Hey, when he comes to you, you don't check with me first, right?"

Hayford shrugged.

"I just don't like it when he knows things I don't know he knows."

"He always knows things you don't know. That's why he's Tony and you're Buie." Castille took the headphones from around his neck and slipped them close to his ears. "You better get going. They're asking where you are."

Thirty-seven

*L*ate that afternoon Scott noticed Doug Corretti's head was beginning to bob lower and lower. The distraction didn't sit well with Somerset.

"Father Scott, are you listening?"

The tone of Somerset's voice caught Scott off guard.

"What? Oh ... Yes." He gave Somerset an amused grin. "Could you repeat the question?"

"I'll remind you this is a deposition ..."

Corretti's eyes fluttered and his chin dropped to his chest. Scott tried not to notice. Somerset saw it this time and caught Larry King's attention.

"Is he all right?"

Before Larry could answer, Corretti opened his eyes.

"Just resting my eyes."

Everyone chuckled. Somerset turned his legal pad to a clean sheet.

"Didn't mean to bore you."

Corretti adjusted his jacket.

"I don't think it could be avoided."

Somerset paused. He had a puzzled look on his face, as if he was unsure how to take the comment. Finally, he turned to Scott.

"Now before all of that I believe we were discussing the number of times Mr. Connolly had been to your church prior to the conversation about the stained-glass windows."

"I can't remember how many times he came. At least once. Maybe more than that."

"So you talked about the windows."

"Yes."

"Now you say the conversation had moved on from Keyton Attaway. What does that mean?"

"Just that we'd moved on to talk about other things. About Mike Connolly. His life. That sort of thing."

"How long had you known Mr. Attaway?"

"Attaway?"

"Yes. Keyton Attaway. How long had you known him?"

"Several years."

"Been to his home?"

"Yes."

"Knew his family? Wife. Children."

"Yes."

"Have you ever visited in Mr. Connolly's home?"

"Mr. Connolly?"

"Yes. Mr. Connolly. You've been to Mr. Attaway's home on various occasions. Have you ever been to Mr. Connolly's?"

"No. I haven't."

"When you smelled alcohol on Mr. Connolly. Those times when you smelled it, would you say he was drunk?"

"I don't know. What do you mean?"

"Could he have driven a car? At the time you recall when you smelled alcohol on him. On those occasions was he sober enough to drive a car?"

"I suppose."

"You suppose. I need you to be sure."

"I don't know if he was over the limit or not."

"You mean the legal limit?"

"Yes. The point one or whatever it is."

"Was he staggering?"

"No."

"Was his speech slurred?"

"No."

"Did he seem confused?"

"No."

"Now in the course of talking with Mr. Connolly about Keyton Attaway, did you ever observe anything about him other than the smell of alcohol?"

"I'm not sure what you mean."

"Well ... Anything. Anything remarkable. Anything out of the ordinary."

"Not really."

"Someone said they heard him talking about seeing Truman Albritton one afternoon, but Truman was already dead that morning before lunch."

"Yes."

"You heard about that? About Mr. Connolly saying he talked to Mr. Albritton that afternoon, but Albritton had died that morning?"

"Yes."

"Did you talk to him about it?"

"Yes."

"Tell us about that."

"He came to my office one day, rather shaken."

"He? Who?"

"Mike. Mike Connolly. He came to my office one day. Told me just what you said. A woman ... Leigh Ann Agostino and Truman Albritton had him cornered in a hangar at Brookley. Another man was there with a gun. About to shoot him. This other man was. Was about to shoot him. They were walking him to the back of this abandoned hangar, and just about the time he thought he would have been shot, Mike turned around to face the man. And he was gone."

"Gone?"

"Gone."

"The man with the gun was gone?"

"All of them."

"All of them? All of them were gone?"

"Gone. The hangar was empty. Except for an airplane. That's what he told me. I wasn't there."

"Whose plane was it?"

"I have no idea. I think he thought they were going to shoot him and leave in the airplane."

"Who was going to shoot him?"

"The man with the pistol."

"He was going to shoot him and get away in the airplane?"

"I think he thought ... I think Mike thought they were all going away. The man with the pistol, the woman, Mr. Albritton."

"Where were they going?"

"As I recall, down to a Caribbean island."

"And what did you say after he told you this? After Mr. Connolly told you this happened. What did you say to him?"

"He had already heard that Truman Albritton was dead. I told him I had heard about it on the news myself. I didn't know about Ms. Agostino."

"But he knew."

"Yes. He knew. She was in the hospital at that point. I think. Something had happened to her earlier in the day."

"Something that would have made it physically impossible for her to be in that hangar at the time he said she was there?"

"Yes."

"Do you now know for a fact that she was not in the hangar?"

"No."

"She was not there?"

"I don't know that she was not there. As far as I know, she was."

"Even though you also know that she was in the hospital before Mr. Connolly was in the hangar."

"Yes."

"How is that possible?"

"How is it possible for me to believe it? Or how is it possible for that to happen?"

"How is it possible for this to happen? Assume what he said is true. Mr. Connolly saw her in the afternoon, but several hours earlier she had been taken to the hospital and according to hospital records was a patient at the hospital at the time he says she was at the hangar?"

"The world you see around you is a lie."

"The world I see around me is a lie?"

"Yes."

Somerset took a deep breath.

"So the world I see, the hospital records I see, the news reports I see, are all a lie, and Mr. Connolly isn't crazy. Or the world I see is true, and Mr. Connolly is either crazy or a liar."

Scott winced.

"That's strong language."

Somerset sighed.

"This is crazy."

"Only if you believe that what you see is all there is."

Somerset made a note on his legal pad.

"Did you know Truman Albritton?"

"I saw him once."

"Where did you see him?"

"In Mike's office."

"You saw him at Mr. Connolly's office?"

"Yes."

"When?"

"Sometime after Mike quit drinking, went through withdrawal."

"He went to rehab?"

"No. He quit on his own. Went home one afternoon. Stopped drinking. His body took care of the rest."

"Must have been rough."

"I'm sure it was."

"So sometime after that, you saw Mr. Albritton at Mr. Connolly's office."

"Yes. I went to his office to see about him. To see about Mike. After what he'd been through."

"What he'd been through?"

"Getting off of alcohol."

"How did you hear about it? How did you know he was drying out?"

"His secretary called me."

"What is her name?"

"Gordon. Myrtice Gordon."

"You know her?"

"I've met her a few times."

"What did Ms. Gordon say about Mr. Connolly and what he'd gone through?"

"Just that he had stopped drinking and needed some help."

"Help? Staying sober?"

"Yes. Getting sober. Staying sober."

"So you went to his office and Mr. Albritton was there."

"Yes."

"What happened?"

"When I got there, Mike had Mr. Albritton by the collar and shoved him against the wall."

"They were fighting?"

"They were ... Well, I didn't see anyone throw a punch, but ... Yes. I'd say they were fighting."

"What were they fighting about?"

"They had been talking about Keyton Attaway. Mr. Albritton said something about Mike being too drunk to defend the man they'd arrested. Maybe he should plead him out and let it go."

"And Mr. Connolly didn't like that."

"He was a little upset by it."

"So Mr. Connolly had him by the collar. What happened after that?"

"Mrs. Gordon hollered at him. At Mike. He let him go. Mr. Albritton left."

"Did Mr. Albritton say anything?"

"I think he said something like, 'You'll regret this.' Or something like that."

"Mr. Albritton said that?"

"Yes."

"And you were there? You personally witnessed this?"

"Yes."

"Did you see Mr. Albritton on any other occasion?"

"No."

"Now you said before that you knew Keyton Attaway and his family. You knew his wife?"

"Yes."

"Were you present at anytime when Mr. Connolly talked to Keyton's wife?"

"Yes."

"You were present when they talked?"

"Yes."

"Tell us about that meeting."

"Not long after the time I saw Mr. Albritton in Mike's office ... In fact, we talked about this when I was there that time."

"After Mr. Albritton left?"

"Yes. Mike had been to see Karen Attaway earlier. I don't know when. Sometime earlier, before the incident at his office with Albritton. And they got into an argument."

"Mr. Connolly and Mrs. Attaway?"

"Yes. They got into an argument and—"

"What kind of an argument?"

"Over Keyton."

"She was mad at Mr. Connolly about it?"

"She threw a glass of tea at him."

"Mrs. Attaway threw it at Mr. Connolly?"

"Yes."

Goolsby chuckled.

"My kind of woman."

Somerset continued.

"How did you find out about this incident? Were you present?"

"I wasn't there. She told me about it. Karen Attaway told me."

"When did she tell you this?"

"I don't remember the exact date."

"Do you keep a diary?"

"A diary?"

"Yes. You know. A journal."

"No."

"Have you ever kept one?"

"No. Not that I recall."

"You don't keep a prayer journal?"

"No."

"But you have a datebook. A calendar."

"No comment."

"You don't get a choice."

"I'm not giving you my calendar. I'm not giving you my date-book. If I later remember that I have a prayer journal, I'm not giving you that."

Somerset stared at Scott.

"You realize you are here under a subpoena."

Carr spoke up.

"Let's stick to the subject."

Somerset gave him a cold look.

"This is my deposition. I'll say what the subject is."

Carr leaned forward and turned toward Somerset.

"John, this is a waste of time. He's a priest. He's not going to give you that kind of information. Judge McKenzie isn't going to let you have it. If any of this leads us anywhere and the dates become relevant, we can fight about it then."

"That's your opinion. This is my deposition."

Carr scooted his chair back from the table.

"Let's go off the record."

Thirty-eight

Chattahoochee was a small town along the shore of Lake Seminole near the Florida-Georgia line. Glover found it without any trouble. He steered the car off the pavement onto the parking lot at Seminole Bait and Tackle, a rambling wooden building crammed between the highway and the lake. He parked the car beneath an oak tree at the corner of the lot and made his way to the front door.

Inside, he found an old man sitting on a ladder-back chair behind a well-worn wooden counter, fanning himself with a folded newspaper. The man looked up as Glover entered.

"You must be lost."

Glover chuckled.

"Why do you say that?"

"'Cause nobody goes fishing dressed like that, and most of my customers are people I know."

Glover nodded.

"Well, I'm not lost. But I do need to ask you some questions."

"You aren't the law."

"No?"

The old man shook his head.

"I can tell."

"How's that?"

"I know things." He tossed the newspaper aside. "What can I do for you?"

Glover took the photograph of Scott Nolan from his pocket and laid it on the counter.

"You ever seen this man before?"

The old man stood and picked up the photo.

"I don't know." He held it close. "Looks familiar, maybe. Who is he?"

"He's a priest."

The old man's eyes brightened.

"A priest?"

"Yes. From Mobile."

The old man stared at the picture.

"Don't get many priests in here."

Glover continued.

"According to records from the phone company, someone made a call from your pay phone to that priest's church."

"When?"

"About a year, year and a half ago."

The old man laid the photograph on the counter.

"I can't remember back that far."

Glover took another photograph from his pocket and handed it to the old man.

"What about her? Ever seen her?"

The old man arched his eyebrows.

"I remember her." He held the photograph by the tips of his fingers. "Pretty lady. Kind of tall, slender. Big, dark eyes. Came in here with a fellow." He laid the picture on the counter. "Where's that one of the priest?"

Glover handed it to him.

"This might have been him. I can't quite remember."

"But you remember the woman."

The old man nodded his head.

"Yeah. They came in here two or three times. I think they were staying across the street."

Glover frowned.

"Across the street?"

"Yeah." The old man gestured over his shoulder. "At the motel."

Glover looked out the window. Across the highway a single-story motel sat back from the road, all but hidden in a grove of tall oaks. A neon sign near the pavement showed the name. Seminole Lodge.

"They were staying there?"

"Yeah. I think so. I saw them go across the highway."

"And you're sure it was her?"

"Yeah." The old man nodded. "I'm sure. She didn't speak very good English. Had a thick accent." He folded his arms across his chest. "She saw my pickle jar." He pointed to a gallon-size glass jar on the counter. "She had a hard time telling me she wanted one." A proud smile lit up his face. "I fished one out for her and gave it to her on a napkin. She enjoyed it so much I didn't even charge her for it."

Thirty-nine

By the time Somerset arranged a conference call with Judge McKenzie, the day was almost gone. Several of the lawyers had chosen not to stick around. Unwilling to give in, Scott waited in the conference room.

When the call came through, Somerset placed a telephone in the center of the table and pressed a button. Judge McKenzie's voice came from the speaker.

"Good afternoon, gentlemen."

"Good afternoon, Your Honor. This is John Somerset. I have you on speaker phone. We're here in my office. A whole room full of lawyers. Too many to introduce everyone, but we're here in Tonsmeyer v. Hayford, trying to finish the deposition of the priest, Father Scott Nolan, and we have another problem."

"What's the issue?"

"In the course of questioning Rev. Nolan, I asked him if he kept a journal or a datebook. He said he doesn't keep a journal, but apparently he does keep a datebook. A calendar."

Judge McKenzie's response was garbled.

"... a calendar."

Somerset spoke up.

"I'm sorry, Your Honor. I was talking at the same time. Could you repeat that?"

Judge McKenzie repeated herself.

"I said, what do you mean by a datebook? Are we talking about a calendar?"

"Yes, Your Honor. A calendar. An appointment book."

"Rev. Nolan?"

Scott responded.

"Yes, Your Honor."

"Do you have anyone there representing you at this deposition?"

"No, Your Honor."

"What's the basis for your refusal to provide them your calendar?"

"Your Honor, we are way far away from anything to do with what I understand this lawsuit to be about. I mean, we've been here all morning, and he's still asking me questions about Keyton Attaway. My appointment book has information about many things, including things about parishioners who have no connection whatsoever to anything remotely connected to this case. I can't let him just ramble through my Day-Timer."

"Mr. Somerset?"

"This is a deposition, Your Honor. I'm allowed a lot of latitude in what I can ask about."

"Do you have a time frame in mind?"

"Well, right now we're talking about things that happened four or five years ago."

"Four or five years? You want me to dig up Day-Timers for the last four or five years and let you plunder through the life of my entire congregation?"

"Your Honor ..."

Once again Judge McKenzie's response was garbled.

"... point."

Somerset stepped in.

"I'm sorry, Your Honor. I was talking at the same time again."

"I said, he has a point."

"I don't see any way around it. I don't see any alternative but to look through all of them."

Scott shook his head.

"This isn't right."

Judge McKenzie responded.

"What's that, Rev. Nolan?"

"This isn't right, Your Honor. It's just not right. He can't go on a fishing expedition like this with a mere witness. And not much of one at that. My sole connection to this case is the fact that I talked to Mike Connolly and developed a pastoral relationship with him over the past several years."

"Mr. Somerset, is Mike Connolly a party to this lawsuit?"

"Mike Connolly?"

"Yes. Is he a party to this lawsuit?"

"No, Your Honor. He's not a party to this lawsuit."

Scott spoke up.

"That's my point, Your Honor. I'm not a party to this lawsuit. Mike Connolly's not a party to this lawsuit. He's questioning me because of my relationship to someone who is not even a party to this case. I'm, like, three steps removed from this thing, and now he wants to delve into the life of my entire church."

"Mr. Somerset, anything further?"

"No, Your Honor."

"Anyone else in the room have anything?"

There was no response.

"No one?"

Somerset answered.

"I don't think so, Your Honor."

"Well, here's my ruling. Mr. Somerset, unless you can narrow down the date to a specific time frame, other than the last five years ... Unless you can come up with some specific dates, I'm not going to let you have those calendars. Rev. Nolan, if he can give you some specific dates, or at least some specific months ... Not every month in the year for the last five years, but some specific months, then we'll set up a time for you to bring those entries for those specific months over to my office, and I'll look at them and see if there is anything in there that I think he's entitled to."

"Yes, Your Honor."

"All right. Have a good day."

Forty

Three days later Scott was back in the conference room at Somerset's office. A few of the faces at the far end of the room were different, but most of the people around the table were the same. The chatter in the room died away as Somerset began.

"All right. Do you know a man named Hollis Toombs?"

"Yes."

"You're smiling."

"You are too."

"Something about Hollis Toombs makes you smile?"

"Something about Hollis Toombs makes God smile."

"Oh? Tell us about him. What do you know about him?"

"He's a guy who lives ... When I first came to know him, he lived in a shack on a bayou in the swamp down around Fowl River."

"Have you ever been to that shack?"

"Once."

"When was that?"

"Hollis was beaten rather badly a year or two ago. Left for dead. Mike found him. Floating in the bayou."

"Who did that to him?"

"I don't know."

"So why were you at Hollis Toombs' shack?"

"I went down there one day after he got out of the hospital. To see if he was all right."

"Is that the only time you've been to his place?"

"Yes."

"Does he still live in that shack on the bayou?"

"No."

"Where does he live now?"

"He has a house on the bay. I'm not sure where. I've never been to it. I think it's down there near Sprinkle's Store."

"On Mobile Bay? A house on Mobile Bay?"

"Yes."

"So he moved out of the shack into a house?"

"Yes."

"What brought that on?"

"He got married."

"When he lived in the shack, what did he do down there?"

"Just lived, I suppose. Hunt. Fish. Mind his own business. You'd have to ask him."

"How did you come to meet him?"

"He's a friend of Mike."

"Mike Connolly?"

"Yes."

"Mike introduced you?"

"As much as you can be introduced to Hollis."

"Tell us about meeting him."

"I don't really recall the first time I met him."

"You said Mr. Connolly introduced you."

"Yes. I mean, I knew him because he does work for Mike, but I don't remember how I came to actually meet him. I came to know Mike and then Hollis was there."

"He does work for Mr. Connolly?"

"Yes."

"What kind of work?"

"Investigates cases for him."

"What cases has he worked on?"

"You'd have to ask Mike about that."

"Well, you said you knew him because he worked on Mike's cases. What cases do you know about that he did work on for Mr. Connolly?"

"I wouldn't know anything about any of that."

"Did any of it involve Buie Hayford or the Tonsmeyer—"

"I wouldn't know. I think he helped him in that case with Joe Ingram's son ..."

"Steve?"

"Yes. Steve Ingram."

"What kind of work?"

"I don't know. I just remember something about him helping with that case."

"All right. What else did he do? What other cases did Hollis Toombs investigate for Mr. Connolly?"

"I don't know. I mean, he helped out with the women at Panama Tan."

"He worked at Panama Tan?"

"No. He helped get them out of the warehouse."

"We'll get to that. What else did he do? What other cases did he work on?"

"He took Mike out to Horn Island. But that was the same case."

"The one with the women from the tanning salon?"

"Yes."

"Hollis has a boat?"

"I don't know."

"How did they get to Horn Island?"

"They rented a boat."

"I thought you said he took Mr. Connolly to Horn Island."

"He arranged a trip out there."

"Was Hollis along on this trip?"

"That's my understanding."

"Were you there?"

"No."

"Whose boat did they go on?"

"A guy named Taylor Harper."

"And how do you know this?"

"Hollis told me. Taylor told me. I think Mike even said something about it."

"You know Taylor Harper?"

"Yes."

"Who is he?"

"He's a charter-boat captain. Has a boat at the marina on Dauphin Island."

"How do you know him?"

"Keyton introduced me to him."

"How did Keyton Attaway know him?"

"Taylor's boat was tied up near Keyton's. He was down there one day when we went fishing. Keyton stopped to talk to him. Introduced me to him. I see him when I'm down there."

"Have you ever been out on his boat?"

"No."

"Had Keyton ever gone out on his boat?"

"On Taylor's boat?"

"Yes."

"I wouldn't know."

"What do you know about Taylor Harper?"

"Not much. His brother used to be the clerk at federal court. I don't know what Taylor did. He's retired. Loved to fish. Bought a boat. Started taking charters."

"Mr. Harper retired and bought a boat?"

"Yes. I think so."

"How old is he?"

"Not very. Maybe my age. Not any older than I."

"Why did he retire?"

"I have no idea. You'd have to ask him."

"What kind of boat does he have?"

"Thirty-four-foot Crusader."

"That's a nice boat."

"Yes."

"You could go most anywhere in that."

"I believe you could."

"But he and Keyton Attaway were friends?"

"Yes."

"Ever see them together other than at the boat?"

"No."

"Okay. Any other—"

"Yes."

"Yes what?"

"I did see them one other time."

"Okay. When was that?"

"That day I told you about. When John Agostino went fishing with us and then we came back and they went to Keyton's beach house and I drove home alone."

"What about it?"

"When they left the marina, Taylor was with them."

"Taylor Harper went to the beach house with them?"

"I don't know if he made it as far as the beach house or where they actually went. But when they left the marina, Keyton said that's where they were going, and Taylor was in the car with them."

"How did he come to be in the car with them?"

"We got back from fishing. Cleaned the fish. Put them on ice. Washed down the boat. We were standing at the back finishing up. Keyton hollered over to Taylor."

"Their boats were that close?"

"Yes. Taylor's boat was two slips down from Keyton's."

"Okay. He hollered over to him. What did Keyton say?"

"He said, 'You about ready?' Or something like that."

"So Taylor already knew what was happening."

"Sounded like it. I mean, far as I know they didn't discuss it any that day. We left before sunup. Taylor wasn't down there when we went out. When we came back in, he was there on his boat, but Keyton and John didn't go over there or say anything to him."

"Just hollered over to him."

"Yes."

"And then they left together."

"Yes. I think Taylor said, 'Waiting on you.' Keyton dried his hands and got out of the boat. John followed him. Keyton looked back at me and said, 'Take all those fish you want. We'll get what's left on our way back.' I said, 'Okay.' Taylor came from his boat, followed them down the dock. They got in Keyton's car and drove away."

"Was this one of those times when Mr. Attaway went down the night before? Maybe he and Judge Agostino spent the night at the beach house?"

"I don't know. I mean, they didn't say anything about it to me. Could have been. They were both at the boat when I got down there."

"Judge Agostino and Keyton Attaway were already at the boat when you arrived that morning?"

"Yes."

"What time was it when you arrived?"

"I'm not sure. It was still dark."

"Did you see anyone else down there? That time. The time we're talking about. When Taylor Harper left with them. That trip. Did you see anyone else down there that you knew or recognized?"

"No."

"Okay. Any other cases you know of that Hollis Toombs worked on for Mike Connolly?"

"No."

Forty-one

*T*hat night at his office Hayford opened the refrigerator in the break room and took out a bottle of ginger ale. He twisted off the top and turned it up for a long drink.

"I thought you were supposed to sip that stuff."

Startled, Hayford turned to see who had spoken. Glover grinned from the doorway. Hayford scowled.

"Where have you been?"

"Working."

"Find anything?"

Glover moved across the room and took a seat at a table.

"The man at the service station in Marianna doesn't remember them."

"What about that bait shop? Castille gave you the name, didn't he?"

Glover nodded.

"The old man who runs it remembers her. Said she came in there with a guy two or three times. He remembered her because she liked his pickles."

A laugh burst from Hayford, sending ginger ale spewing from his mouth.

"His what?"

Glover chuckled.

"His pickles."

Hayford continued to laugh. Glover leaned back in the chair.

"He had a pickle jar on the counter. She asked about them. He gave her one."

Hayford took a seat at the table.

"What were they doing there?"

"They stayed at a motel across the highway. Seminole Lodge. I talked to the couple that run it. They had a card for the room where they checked in, but it didn't have anything on it. Just the room number, a date."

"How'd they pay for it?"

"Cash."

"That's it?"

"They remembered her because she was pretty and because the wife cleaned the rooms. She came in on them one morning."

Glover paused. Hayford arched an eyebrow.

"And what was the good priest doing?"

"He was asleep on the floor."

Hayford's shoulders slumped.

"The floor?"

Glover nodded.

"She was sleeping in the bed. He was sleeping on the floor."

"That doesn't help us."

"Neither does this. While they were there, two men came to see them. Spent most of the day in the room with them. Spent the night. The next day, another guy and a woman arrived. They joined them in the room. Late that afternoon, the man and woman took her with them."

"Any idea who it was?"

"They think it was the FBI. Men had short haircuts. Gray suits."

"How'd they pay for the extra room?"

"Rooms. That's the other reason they remembered. They rented more rooms than usual. All-night rooms."

Hayford frowned.

"All-night rooms?"

Glover nodded.

"Apparently most of their business is by the hour."

Hayford took a sip of ginger ale.

"So it's a dead end."

"I guess. We could get the records from that pay phone and see where the calls were made to. Might show something interesting." A puzzled look wrinkled Glover's forehead. "Wonder why he called from a pay phone?"

"Probably trying to fix it so the call couldn't be traced back to him."

"So how'd we find out about it?"

Hayford smiled.

"He made a mistake. He called his office."

Forty-two

*T*he room fell silent as Somerset entered. He set a cup of coffee on the table and took a seat. When everyone was ready, he turned to Scott.

"Okay. Let's keep moving. Now, Hollis Toombs. What else do you know about him?"

"Not much. He was in the Marines during Vietnam. Intelligence. Spent a lot of time doing things he can't talk about or won't talk about. Maybe things we don't want to know about."

"In Vietnam?"

"Yes."

"Lot of people would like to forget what happened in that war. What else do you know about him?"

"He was sort of burned out after Vietnam. Came back. Moved to the swamp."

"Did he buy this place where he was living? Was he a squatter?"

"Inherited it from his uncle."

"Inherited it?"

"Yes. I think that's how he met Mike. Some kind of squabble with the family over the uncle's will. Mike represented him on it. They won. Hollis got several hundred acres in the swamp. And Mike got a friend."

"And an investigator."

"Yes. I guess so."

"What was the uncle's name? Do you know?"

"I have no idea."

"Where did he grow up? Hollis. Did Hollis grow up around here?"

"I think he was from Irvington. Maybe St. Elmo. I'm not sure.

Somewhere around there."

"Ever notice anything strange about him?"

"About Hollis?"

"Yes."

"Everything about Hollis is strange."

"What do you mean?"

"He laughs when most people would cry. Sees the humor in otherwise tragic circumstances. He charges when most would retreat. He's just not your average guy."

"Ever seen him drunk?"

"No. Never seen him drink, either."

"Spend any time alone with him? I mean, when Mr. Connolly wasn't around?"

"Yes."

"Where was that?"

"Cape San Blas."

"Where is that?"

"Florida. Over around Port St. Joe."

"What was over there?"

"A house."

"Whose house?"

"Belongs to Rick Connolly. Mike's brother."

"Rick lives there?"

"No. He lives in Birmingham. This was a summer house. Beach house."

"Who all was there?"

"The women. Me. Hollis Toombs. Mrs. Gordon."

"The women? What women?"

"The women from Panama Tan."

"Tell me about it. Tell me about going over there with Hollis."

"After they took the women from the warehouse, we moved them to Rick's beach house."

"The warehouse?"

"They were living in a warehouse. Down there by those old banana warehouses."

"The women were in a banana warehouse?"

"No. Just down there by them. In that area. The building they were in was a little further up."

"All right. We'll get to the warehouse in a minute. They took them. Who is 'they'?"

"Hollis and Mike."

"Okay. Go ahead. After Hollis Toombs and Mike Connolly took the women from the warehouse. What then?"

"I drove them over in the church van. Over to Rick's beach house on Cape San Blas. Hollis went with me. I stayed over there long enough to get them settled. Spent a night, or maybe two. Then I came back. He stayed with them."

"Mr. Connolly didn't go?"

"No. He came over later."

"Why didn't he go with them when they went over?"

"He had other things to take care of, I guess."

"Such as?"

"I don't know. Maybe it wasn't that at all. One of the women was interested in him. I don't think he wanted to be over there where she was. But I don't know. I'm just guessing."

"This woman has a name?"

"The woman who was interested in him?"

"Yes."

"Raisa."

"Spell it."

"R-A-I-S-A."

"Rasa."

"Rah-*ee*-sa. Sounds sort of like Louisa."

"Raisa."

"Yes."

"Know her last name?"

"No."

"Are the women still there? Over at Cape San Blas."

"No."

"Where are they now?"

"Everywhere. I guess."

"Where, exactly?"

"I don't know. They were resettled in various places."

"You stayed with them the entire time they were there?"

"No. I stayed a day or two, then went home."

"Hollis stayed there with them by himself?"

"Mrs. Gordon was there."

"Myrtice Gordon? Mr. Connolly's secretary?"

"Yes."

"You and Mr. Toombs talked while you were at this place with the women?"

"Yes."

"What did you talk about?"

"He was interested in one of the women. We talked about her."

"What was her name?"

"Victoria. I'm not sure that's actually her real first name. But that's the name she goes by. Victoria Verchinko."

"Spell it, please."

"V-E-R-C-H-I-N-K-O."

"What did he say about her?"

"Just the kinds of things a man says about a woman when he's interested in her."

"What specifically?"

"We talked about what they'd been through. How it might affect her. How she was from a different country. Didn't speak much English. Would that be a problem. Things like that."

"Did they have sex?"

"Not to my knowledge. Not while we were there."

"Is this the woman he married? I think you said something earlier about a honeymoon."

"Yes. They married."

"Did you perform the wedding?"

"No."

"Did you attend the wedding?"

"No."

"How many women did you have with you when you were over there at the beach house?"

"Eleven. I think."

"And they've all been resettled?"

"Yes."

"Who resettled them?"

"The State Department."

"How did that work?"

"Mike set it up. I don't know who he called."

"Did anyone from the State Department talk to you?"

"Yes."

"To whom did you speak?"

"I don't remember her name."

"What did she talk to you about?"

"She wanted to verify some of the details. Where they worked. Where they lived. Were they being coerced."

"And you told her?"

"I told her about seeing the tanning salon. About what the women said. Where they were being kept."

"You saw the tanning salon?"

"Yes."

"Do you know where any of these women are located now?"

"Raisa is somewhere in Bosnia."

"She went home?"

"She went back to testify against the man who set her up."

"Set her up?"

"Yes. She was approached by a man in Bosnia who told her he could get her into the movie business. Entertainment business. That's how she got over here."

"Is that what she was doing here?"

"No. By the time I knew her, she had been forced to become a prostitute."

"Did she tell you how that happened? What it was they did to her that forced her to do something like that?"

"No."

"What about the others? Where are they now?"

"They're here in the United States, I assume. I think that was the way it worked out. They all got to stay."

"Are they in a protection program? Like a witness protection program?"

"I can't say."

"Are you saying it's against the law for you to disclose information about them?"

"I'm saying I'm not talking about that."

Somerset lowered his head as if staring down at the legal pad on the table before him. Hayford whispered something in his ear.

Forty-three

All day long Hayford sat at the conference table and listened as Scott talked about the women at the tanning salon, housed in a warehouse, liberated by Mike Connolly and Hollis Toombs. With each answer to each question he felt the tension rising. None of the women knew anything about him. They knew Manny Fernandez. They knew Pete Rizutto and that guy with the oily hair who drove him around. Every one of them had sex with Ford Defuniak and Perry Braxton. But they didn't even know Hayford existed. Except for Tatiana. She didn't know much, but what she saw was far more lethal than anything any of the others knew, and with each word out of Scott's mouth Hayford saw her face.

When they finished for the day, Somerset stood to leave. Hayford took his arm.

"Let's talk."

Somerset checked his watch.

"It's kind of late. I have someplace to be in an hour."

Hayford exploded.

"I'm paying you a lot of money for your time. The least you could do is talk to me."

The lawyers still in the room stared at them. All the color vanished from Somerset's face.

"Wait for me in my office."

Hayford pushed the chair out of the way and walked down the hall. He paced back and forth in Somerset's office, hands in his pockets, muttering to himself.

In a few minutes Somerset entered.

"That wasn't a good idea."

"What?"

"Yelling at me in there."

"I'm paying you. I expect to be able to talk to you."

"You've talked to me. You talk to me every day. You pass me notes every two minutes. You bend my ear when we take a break." Somerset took a seat behind his desk. "Shouting at me only tells them something is getting to you. We want them in a settling mood on this case." He leaned back in the chair. "For as little money as possible."

"I'm not worried about the insurance company's money."

"What are you worried about?"

"I'm worried about the missing woman."

"We'll get to her."

"You're taking a mighty long time."

"These things take time. You know that. You've taken plenty of depositions. You can't just walk in there with a sledgehammer and beat it out of them."

"A good beating might help his memory."

Somerset leaned forward.

"Buie, if you talk like that again, I'll resign from this case." He pointed to a chair. "Sit down."

"I like standing."

Somerset shouted.

"Sit down. Now."

Hayford took his hands from his pockets and sat. Somerset looked at him for a moment.

"What could that woman tell them that Hollis Toombs' wife couldn't?"

Somerset waited for an answer. Hayford frowned.

"What?"

"Victoria Verchinko. She lived at the warehouse. She worked in the tanning salon. What could this other woman tell them that Verchinko couldn't?"

Hayford dropped his gaze to the floor.

"It isn't just about me."

"Oh?"

"Victoria Verchinko wouldn't know me if she saw me. She doesn't know my name. Doesn't know I exist."

"And this other woman does?"

Hayford leaned back and crossed his legs. Somerset took a pen from his jacket and scribbled a note.

"I thought all any of these women could talk about was the nature of the business in that building. I mean, that's the whole point of putting any of them on the stand. To show how the property was being used." He leaned back in his chair again. "Isn't that all they can talk about, Buie?"

Hayford stood.

"We need to find the other woman. That priest knows where she is." Hayford pointed at Somerset. "It's your job to make him talk."

Forty-four

The next morning Somerset picked up where he'd ended the previous day.

"Now you and Hollis Toombs drove the women from the tanning salon over to Cape San Blas. Back up to the beginning of that and tell us what you did. How did you get involved?"

"Mike came to my house one Saturday night. Told me he needed to get a message to one of the women at the tanning salon. Asked me if I would take it to her."

"And you agreed?"

"Yes."

"Why? Why you?"

"He said he didn't have any other way to do it."

"Okay. He asked you. What happened next?"

"I asked him what he wanted me to tell her. He told me. I went down there."

"What did he want you to tell her?"

"For her and the other women to meet him on the street behind the warehouse."

"Do you know where this warehouse is located?"

"I do now."

"You didn't then? At the time he asked you, you didn't know where it was?"

"Correct."

"How did you come to know where it is?"

"I went down there."

"How did you know where to go?"

"Mike told me sort of where it was. The general area. Hollis told me how to find it."

"While you were on this trip with these women? This was one of the things you talked about?"

"Yes."

"Ever been inside? Inside the warehouse?"

"No."

"Do you know anyone else who knows where it is? Other than Hollis Toombs, Mike Connolly, and the women you ... took on this trip?"

"No."

"Do you know who owns it?"

"The warehouse?"

"Yes."

"No."

"You don't know who owns the warehouse?"

"No."

"Anyone ever tell you who owns it?"

"No."

"When you went down there. When you drove by the warehouse, did you stop? Get out?"

"No. I just drove by."

"What time of day was it?"

"Afternoon, I think."

"See anyone around there?"

"No."

"Ever talk to anyone about this case? The one about the women in the warehouse?"

"Hollis and Mike and I talked a few times about it."

"Anyone else?"

"Not that I can recall."

"Talk to your wife?"

"No."

"You didn't explain to her where you'd been?"

"No."

"She wasn't curious?"

"I don't know."

"What did Hollis and Mike say about it? About this case. You said you'd talked to them about this case. What did they say about it?"

"About the women and ... all that?"

"Yes. About the case with the women and the tanning salon and the warehouse."

Scott pointed to young Sarah Braxton.

"Does she have to be in here?"

"Who? Sarah?"

"Yes."

Doug Corretti nodded.

"Perhaps it would be best if she waited outside."

Somerset glanced over at the court reporter.

"Let's go off the record for just a minute."

Forty-five

Castille left Pate to monitor the deposition and returned to the war room at Hayford's office. As he entered, Blake Nicholas looked up with a wide grin.

"We've got something."

"What is it?"

The look on Nicholas' face turned serious.

"Phone calls to the priest's house. First one came last night. Took us awhile to track it down, but it came from a phone in Orlando."

"How long was it?"

"Not very. Answering machine picked up. Caller hung up."

"And?"

Nicholas grinned once more.

"Early this morning, there was another. Listen to this."

He pressed a button on the keyboard. There was a beep, then a voice.

"I need to ..."

Castille frowned.

"That's it?"

"Yeah. Not much, but it sounds like a—"

Castille interrupted.

"Play it again."

Nicholas pressed a key. The voice played again. Castille nodded.

"Again."

The voice played once more. Castille took a cell phone from his pocket.

"Where was this one from?"

"Same area. Orlando."

"Different number?"

"Yeah."

Castille punched in a number on his cell phone.

"You checked it out?"

"Cell phone. Both of them."

"Both of them?"

Nicholas nodded.

"If you're calling Glover, he said he was going to Auburn. He probably turned his phone off."

Castille shook his head.

"Need some muscle for this one."

He turned away and spoke into the cell phone.

"Hey. It's me. We have something."

A moment later he switched off the phone and shoved it in his pocket. He slapped Nicholas on the back.

"Good work."

Forty-six

With Sarah out of the room, Somerset continued.

"You were about to tell us what Hollis and Mike Connolly said about this case. About the case with the women from the tanning salon."

"They said Ford Defuniak and the other guy ... The one driving the car. They said they got off easy."

"What else did they say?"

"They said Camille Braxton should have shot her husband instead of throwing him out. They said ..."

"Who said that?"

"Hollis."

"What else did he say?"

"I don't remember the exact words."

"He blamed Perry Braxton? Thought he was at fault?"

"As between the two of them. Perry and his wife, yes."

"What about Perry Braxton and the women at the tanning salon? Did they have anything to say about that? Did Hollis Toombs or Mike Connolly say anything about whether Braxton was involved with those women?"

"Not them. Hollis and Mike never said one way or the other about Mr. Braxton and those women."

"Not them. Who did? Did someone else say something about Perry Braxton being involved with the women at the tanning salon?"

"Some of the women."

"Who? Which ones?"

"I don't know their names. Most of them didn't speak English very well."

"So how were you able to talk to them?"

"Raisa interpreted for them."

"So you had a conversation with them where they were talking about Perry Braxton and Raisa was interpreting?"

"Yes."

"When did you have this conversation?"

"While we were over there at the beach house. At Cape San Blas."

"What brought this up?"

"We were sitting around late one afternoon. Hollis said something to me about Perry Braxton. Raisa made a comment about him. One of the other women asked a question. She made a comment. Raisa interpreted it for us. Then the others chimed in and it went from there."

"They knew him by name?"

"His first name. Hollis was talking about him. I don't think he mentioned his name at first. Raisa asked who he was. Hollis described him. Mike had told her his name. She knew his first name. She might have seen a picture of him at some point. I can't remember."

"Someone over there had a picture of Perry Braxton?"

"No. Earlier. Mike or Hollis or someone might have showed her a picture of him while all this was going on. While Mike was working on the case."

"This woman. Raisa. She knew Perry Braxton by his first name?"

"Yes."

"What did she say about him?"

"I'm not sure who said what. They talked about how often he came to the tanning salon. The kinds of things he wanted them to do."

"What kinds of things?"

"Some of it was a little rough, I think."

"He was there frequently?"

"Yes."

"Did they say anything else?"

"Raisa talked about seeing a woman in the car one day."

"Who was it? Who was the woman?"

"His wife."

"She knew Camille Braxton?"

"I don't think so."

"How did she know she was his wife? How was Raisa able to talk about Camille if she didn't know her?"

"Somewhere in the course of all this, Mike showed Raisa a picture of her. A picture of Mrs. Braxton, and she recognized her from that."

"He showed her two pictures? A picture of Perry and one of Camille?"

"I have a vague recollection that it was a picture of both of them together."

"Mr. Connolly was there at the beach house when this conversation took place?"

"No. Sometime before we were talking to her at the beach house. Sometime before that, Mike had shown her a picture."

"So she was recounting this in the conversation we were talking about."

"Yes."

"Go ahead. Tell us what she said about seeing Camille in the car."

"She said she didn't look too good. Camille was slumped against the door. Apparently unconscious. There was blood on the window. Perry looked upset."

"Why was he there with her? With Camille. Where did Raisa see him?"

"At the tanning salon. One morning. As they were coming in. As they were being brought into the tanning salon, this car pulled up. Perry Braxton was driving. Camille was inside."

"This is what these women told you?"

"Yes."

"Why was Camille with him? With Mr. Braxton. Why was she in the car?"

"I don't know. They didn't say."

"Was that the only time Raisa had seen her there?"

"No."

"What were those other times? How many times had she seen Camille there?"

"I'm not sure how many times there were. You'd have to ask her."

"Just tell me what she said. Tell me what Raisa said about it during that conversation you were having with her and Hollis and the other women. What she said about seeing Camille at the tanning salon. The other times."

"She told me about seeing Camille one morning in the car with her husband. Then she told me about seeing her there one other day. Before that day when she was in the car."

"When was that?"

"I don't know the exact date. Just sometime before that morning when she was in the car."

"Earlier that day, or some other day?"

"Some other day."

"What happened? That other time. The earlier time. What happened?"

"She said Camille Braxton came—"

"She spoke about her by name?"

"No."

"How did you know her name?"

"Mike told me. When he and I talked about her. About this case. He used her name. I saw a picture of her. Like I said, I think it was one of them together."

"Of Camille and Perry?"

"Yes. With their daughter. The girl who was in here."

"Have you ever seen them in person? Camille, Perry, Sarah. Have you seen any of them in person?"

"No. I saw the girl, Sarah, when we started this deposition the other day. Whenever that was."

"Okay. This woman. Raisa. She was telling you about seeing a woman you've identified for us as Camille at the tanning salon."

"Yes."

"Go ahead. Tell us what she said."

"She said Camille came there."

"As a customer?"

"Yes."

"Okay."

"They have tanning beds in the front. I guess some people go there just for a tan. I don't know."

"You've seen these beds? These tanning beds."

"Yes."

"Okay."

"So Camille came there as a customer. The man who works there. Manny. He saw her wandering around. Raisa came from one of the rooms in back with a customer. Manny asked Camille what she wanted. Camille said she was looking for a tanning booth. He took her up front to one of the tanning beds."

"Raisa saw this?"

"Yes."

"Who was the customer with Raisa?"

"I don't know."

"You didn't ask?"

"No. She probably wouldn't have known his name anyway."

"Did she have anything else to say?"

"Camille?"

"No. Raisa. In the conversation with you and Hollis and the other women sitting around the beach house that afternoon. Did she have anything else to say?"

"I don't remember anything else right now."

Forty-seven

*T*he next morning Somerset pulled Hayford aside as he entered the office.

"We have to talk." He opened the door to his office and pointed. "Hurry up. Before someone gets here."

Hayford trudged into Somerset's office. Somerset closed the door.

"Why is the FBI calling me?"

Hayford gave him a blank look.

"The FBI?"

"Yeah. The Federal Bureau of Investigation. Federal, Buie. Federal. They called me at home last night. They came by my house. They were there again this morning."

Hayford shrugged.

"It's just harassment, John. They know we have a chance to find out some things that will help me if they go for an indictment. They just want to—"

Somerset raised an eyebrow.

"Oh, I think they're going after an indictment all right."

"What do you mean?"

"They were asking me about a woman. Tatiana Perovic." He glared at Hayford. "That name ring a bell with you, Buie?"

Somerset moved behind the desk. Hayford took a seat.

"Look, John, everything you know about her is something I told you. They can't make you tell them. They're just—"

Somerset held up his hand.

"They don't want to know what you told me. They want to know where she is."

Hayford did his best to keep from smiling.

"Hey, if I knew that, I wouldn't be sitting here."

Somerset frowned.

"What do you mean?"

"It's just an expression, John. Look, I haven't seen her. I haven't done anything with her. I don't know where she is." He sighed. "Relax."

Somerset dropped onto his chair. He tapped the desktop with his finger.

"They say she's a federal witness." He waited for Hayford to look at him. "And she's missing."

Hayford sighed and leaned back in the chair.

"Well, I don't know anything about where she is."

Somerset rested his elbows on the desk and leaned forward.

"Let me tell you something, Buie. I don't mind defending you on this lawsuit. I'll take all the depositions you want. Go to court. File motions. Take it to trial. Work this case to death. But I'm not lying, and I'm not going to jail. Not for you. Not for anyone else."

Hayford ran his hand across his cheek.

"No one's going to jail, John."

Forty-eight

 B y the time Scott came from the elevator that morning, most of the lawyers were already in the conference room. He paused at a table near the door and poured himself a cup of coffee. He took a sip and watched through the doorway as everyone took their places in the same chairs they'd sat in since the first day.

"Just like church," he whispered to himself.

He took another sip, then moved through the doorway to his chair at the end of the table. Moments later Somerset began.

"All right. Now you've told us a few things Mr. Connolly said. You've referred to them in telling us about the other things I've asked you. For instance, he showed you pictures?"

"Yes."

"He told you names?"

"Yes."

"He told you something about where the warehouse was located."

"Yes."

"Where did this conversation take place? Was this one, single conversation?"

"I don't know how many conversations there were."

"Of the ones you remember, where did they take place?"

"After I got back from taking the women to the beach house, I went to his house. To Mike's house. He and I sat around there a little while, talking."

"I thought you said earlier you'd never been to his residence."

"Yes. I think I did say that. I was wrong."

"How many times have you been there?"

"Other than this one time I just mentioned, I can't think of any other times."

"Are there any other of your answers to this deposition you need to correct?"

"None that I know of."

"This conversation you had at Mr. Connolly's house. This occurred on the day you returned from Cape San Blas?"

"Yes."

"What time of the day was it?"

"Early afternoon."

"Tell me about this conversation. What did you and Mr. Connolly talk about?"

"He thanked me for taking the women to the beach house. Asked me if they were all right. I asked him a few questions about where they were living. Were they really in a warehouse. Who did something like that. That sort of thing."

"What did he say?"

"He said the man who'd tried to kill him was the guy behind the whole deal."

"The man who tried to kill him?"

"Yeah. I'm not sure of his name. Something like Rizugo?"

Goolsby spoke up.

"Rizutto."

Scott nodded.

"Yes. Rizutto."

"Mr. Connolly said someone named Rizutto was behind everything?"

"Yeah. He was the one who actually ran the thing. Got the women. Located a place for them to work. Set them up."

"Did he mention the bank? Tidewater National Bank. Did Mr. Connolly ever mention anything about Tidewater in talking about this case? This case with the women."

"No."

"Did he mention Buie Hayford?"

"No."

"Did he mention the trust? The Tonsmeyer Family Trust."

"No. I don't think so."

"What else did he say?"

"Not much, really. Just talk. You know. Did we have enough money. Were they set. That sort of thing."

"Now you mentioned conversations with Hollis and Mr. Connolly. Did you have a conversation with them together about this case?"

"Yes."

"When did that take place?"

"After Hollis came back, I was over at—"

"Wait a minute. Was this a separate incident from the one you remembered awhile ago?"

"Yes, I guess it was. Hollis was still over there. So I guess this is one more time at Mike's house."

"Have you been there any other times other than the time when you came back from taking the women to the beach house and then this later time after Hollis came back?"

"No. Not that I recall."

"What did you see in the house? Were you inside?"

"Yes. I was inside. I didn't see much of anything. Just a house. Living room. Kitchen. I didn't get any farther than the living room."

"No wine bottles sitting on the kitchen counter?"

"No."

"Did you look? Did you go in the kitchen?"

"You can see from the entryway. I didn't see any."

"Okay. When you had this conversation there at Mr. Connolly's residence ... After you returned from driving the women. Was he sober?"

"Yes."

"Did you smell alcohol on him?"

"No."

"He wasn't staggering?"

"No."

"His speech wasn't slurred?"

"No."

"Okay. You were about to tell us about another conversation. After Hollis returned."

"Yes. I dropped by Mike's house one afternoon sometime after Hollis returned. He was there."

"Hollis was there?"

"Yes. They were there. Talking. We all sat around there a few minutes."

"What did they say?"

"This is all just random stuff I'm trying to remember. I can't really recall anything specific right now."

"You walked in. They greeted you. What did you say?"

"Hollis made some crack about me going to the tanning salon. I reminded Mike that he still owed me for it. Mike took out some money and paid me. There was some more banter back and forth. I said whoever put those women in there should be in prison."

"What did Mr. Connolly say to that?"

"I don't recall."

"Mr. Connolly say anything else?"

"I can't recall anything specific right now."

Forty-nine

At noon Hayford took the elevator to the lobby and walked down the street to the Essex Hotel. A downtown landmark, the Essex stood at the corner of Royal Street and St. Michael. Hayford entered from the St. Michael Street side.

The hotel lobby had a marble floor and smooth plaster walls. A crystal chandelier hung near the center of the room, suspended from the ceiling three floors above. Beneath it water gurgled from a fountain. An old man in a gray suit sat on a bench near the fountain. A woman and a small child stood to the left, near the elevators.

Hayford crossed the lobby and stepped inside the lounge. Glover was seated at a table in the corner. Hayford caught the bartender's eye as he moved toward the table.

"How about a Dewar's and water?"

The bartender nodded and reached for a bottle. Hayford slid onto a chair across from Glover.

"What are you working on?"

"Nothing that can't wait."

"Good."

The bartender set the drink on the table. When he was gone, Hayford continued.

"Somerset says the FBI's been asking him questions."

Glover pointed to the glass in front of Hayford.

"You falling off the wagon?"

Hayford scoffed.

"If I'm going to prison, I'm not going sober."

Glover picked up a glass and took a sip. Hayford hadn't noticed the drink before. He pointed to the glass.

"What's that?"

Glover took another sip.

"Vodka Collins."

There was a twinkle in Hayford's eye.

"You old enough for that?"

Glover smiled.

"What's the FBI asking Somerset?"

Hayford took a sip of his drink.

"Looks like they've lost Tatiana."

Glover had a puzzled look.

"Lost her?"

"She got away. They came to Somerset's house last night. Again this morning. Asking him if he knew where she was."

Glover smiled.

"If she's gone, your troubles are over."

"If she leaves and goes away, maybe. But I'm thinking she can't do that."

"Why not?"

"No driver's license. No social security number. Government has this country all locked up now. You can't go to the bathroom without two forms of ID."

"She could always go back to her line of work."

Hayford shrugged.

"Yeah. I suppose. Be a little risky for her. Just out there on the street. She might know about sex for money, but she doesn't know about walking the street."

"Someone would take her in."

Hayford took another sip of his drink.

"Maybe. But I'm thinking she's going to contact the priest."

Glover nodded.

"Castille has all the phones covered."

Hayford shook his head.

"I don't trust Castille."

Glover had a questioning look.

"What's wrong?"

"Just don't trust him." Hayford took another sip. "I'm thinking this woman is coming here."

"Here?"

"Yeah."

"I need you to watch for her."

"Watch for her?"

Hayford nodded.

"I'm thinking this lady is on a low budget. Riding the bus. Maybe hitchhiking." He drained the bottom of his glass and turned to the bar. He gestured with the glass, then turned back to Glover. "Get some people. Your own people. Cover the bus station. The house. The office. Wherever the priest hangs out. Make sure they stay out of sight and make sure Castille doesn't know about it."

The bartender set another glass on the table. Hayford downed it in a single gulp.

Fifty

*S*omerset took a sip of coffee and looked up at Scott.

"All right, Father Scott. We've gotten a little off track from where we started. Mr. Connolly asked you to take a message to one of the women at the tanning salon. What did you do?"

"I went down there. Gave her the message."

"Walk us through it. You drove down there. Parked the car in front."

"In back. I parked in back."

"What day was this?"

"Saturday. Late Saturday afternoon. Almost dark."

"Okay. You parked in back. Went inside. What happened?"

"I went inside. This woman came out. Raisa. I didn't know who she was before. I mean, I knew a name. But I didn't know what she looked like. I'd never met her at that point. She came out. Several more women came into the room."

"Okay. What happened next?"

"Raisa told me to choose the one I wanted. I chose her."

"You knew who she was before you went in there?"

"No. Like I said. I only knew her name. Mike described her to me. Told me she would be the one in charge. And if I couldn't figure out who she was, I could ask for her."

"So you chose her. Then what?"

"Then we went down the—"

"Just a minute. What?"

Hayford interrupted.

"I think—"

Somerset cut him off.

"Wait a minute." He caught the court reporter's eye. "Let's go off the record."

Fifty-one

That evening Castille came to Hayford's office. Hayford was seated at his desk. Castille leaned against the doorframe and folded his arms across his chest.

"Where's Glover?"

Hayford glanced up from the file in his lap and checked his watch.

"Class, I guess."

Castille sauntered from the doorway and flopped onto a chair.

"Did he really fail the bar exam twice?"

"Yeah."

Castille chuckled.

"Think he'll pass it this time?"

Hayford answered without looking up.

"I think so." He turned the page in the file and looked over at Castille. "You need something?"

"I need to send Glover to Florida."

Hayford shook his head.

"He's working on something for me."

"I need him."

"Can't have him."

Castille sat up and leaned toward the desk.

"Buie?"

Hayford looked at him. Castille looked serious.

"I need to send him to Florida."

Hayford returned the look.

"Andre, you can't have him."

Castille leaned back.

"Fine. I'll use my own people."

"That's what you're supposed to be doing anyway. And the next time you think about calling Tony before you call me, think about who's paying you."

Castille shoved himself up from the chair and stormed out.

Fifty-two

*T*he next morning Scott was at Somerset's office early. Somerset was seated behind his desk. Scott leaned through the doorway.

"Any idea how much longer this is going to go on?"

Somerset shrugged.

"I think we're just getting to the good stuff."

Scott didn't like the sound of his voice.

"I'm not trying to be a jerk. I have a job, a congregation. They expect me to be around at least part of the time."

Somerset nodded.

"Probably take another day or two."

Scott turned away. Somerset's assistant moved past him carrying a small paper sack.

"Rev. Nolan, would you like a biscuit? I bought an extra one."

Scott smiled.

"Sure, thanks."

He sat in the conference room and ate.

Thirty minutes later the lawyers began to arrive. Before long Somerset entered and took a seat at the end of the table, across from Scott. Hayford joined him. When everyone was in place, Somerset began again.

"Okay, now. Did you see any women there at the tanning salon that night that weren't in the group you took from the warehouse later?"

"I didn't take anyone from the warehouse."

"You said you took them someplace."

"I picked them up from Mrs. Gordon's house."

"Okay. Did you see any women at the tanning salon that you didn't see at the house?"

"Yes."

"How many?"

"One."

"Do you know her name?"

"Not at the time. I didn't know her name then. I think she was Elsa."

"Someone told you her name later?"

"Yes. I heard Raisa talking about her. Later."

"With whom? Who was she talking to about her?"

"Barbara."

"Barbara?"

"Mike's wi— Ex-wife. Barbara. Barbara Connolly."

"When did Raisa talk to Barbara?"

"Sunday. That Sunday I came with the van to get them."

"Where did you pick them up?"

"Mrs. Gordon's house."

"And Barbara was there, at Mrs. Gordon's house?"

"Yes."

"What was she doing there? Why was she there?"

"She took them shopping."

"She took who shopping?"

"The women. The women from the tanning salon. When Mike and Hollis picked them up behind the warehouse they were still dressed from work."

"What were they wearing?"

"I don't know. I wasn't there."

"What were they wearing the night you went in the tanning salon?"

"Lingerie. A lot of Spandex."

"So that's what they were wearing when they came from the warehouse?"

"I don't know. I just know they said they didn't have much to wear in public. Mrs. Gordon called Barbara. Barbara came over. Took them shopping. Got them some clothes. They weren't dressed that way when I picked them up."

"Mrs. Gordon knew Barbara well enough to call her and ask her to come help with a houseful of women her ex-husband took from a warehouse?"

"I guess so. She called. Barbara came."

"Where did they go shopping?"

"I don't know. I didn't ask."

"Other than ... Elsa, did you see any women at the tanning salon that you didn't later see at the house when you picked them up in the van?"

"No."

"Did you see anyone else at the tanning salon? Besides Raisa, Elsa, the other women who worked there. Did you see anyone else there?"

"Yes."

"Who?"

"I'm not sure. There was a ... customer there."

"Okay. Tell me what happened. You chose Raisa."

"I chose Raisa. The other women moved down a hall behind me. I followed Raisa down the hall in the opposite direction. She took me to a little room. Like a booth. Not even half as big as this room. No windows. Just the one door in and out. She opened the door and motioned for me to go inside. The door opened toward me. Into the hall. As I turned to go in, I saw a man come from a room behind her, farther down the hall. He glanced at me, then turned away and walked out a door at the end of the hall."

"That was a door outside?"

"Yes."

"Did you get a good look at him?"

"Briefly."

"Who was he?"

"He had on a baseball cap. And as he turned away, he put on a pair of sunglasses."

"I thought you said this was at night."

"It was. It was late in the afternoon when Mike came to my house. Almost sunset. It was dark by the time I got down there. To the salon. But he put on sunglasses as he started outside."

"Who was he?"

"It was just a glance."

"But you saw who it was. Who was he?"

"I didn't get a real clear look at him."

"Does your wife know what you did? Does she know you went to that tanning salon?"

"Yes. She knows about this part."

"You told her?"

"Yes."

"What did she think of it?"

"She wasn't too happy I went down there, but we talked about it. She wasn't mad. She understood."

"Did she meet any of these ladies?"

"No. Not that I know of."

"Did you talk to her about them?"

"Only just that I went there to deliver a message. I delivered it and left."

"Did you discuss any of this case with your wife when you returned from wherever you took the women?"

"No."

"She wasn't curious?"

"Yes. She was curious. I told her I couldn't tell her right then. That nothing was wrong. I just couldn't talk."

"And she was okay with that?"

"Yes."

"Have you ever done anything like this before?"

"No."

"Describe the interior of the building again. The tanning salon. You came in the back door?"

"Yes. The back door opens to a little entry area. Then there's a second door that takes you down a hall. The hall turns left and you're in a room. Not as large as this one but big enough for ten or fifteen people. If you stand with your back to the hallway that comes in from the back door, there's another hall to the left and one to the right that runs from that room. The hall we went down was to the left."

"What's down there to the right?"

"To the right?"

"Yes."

"I didn't go down there. I could just see a little of it from where I was."

"What did you see?"

"There was a room with a door open. I could see what looked like a tanning bed inside."

"When you left the building, which way did you go?"

"You mean after I talked to Raisa?"

"Yes. When you were finished with whatever you did at the salon, which way did you go out?"

"I went out the door at the end of the hall."

"The same door you came in?"

"No. There's a door at the end of the hall where the rooms are. A second back door."

"The same one you saw someone, a man, go out?"

"Yes."

"You've referred to a 'back door' and now a 'second back door.' Was there a front door?"

"Yes."

"Where was it?"

"When you come in the back door ... When you park in back, there's a door. It's painted black and ... There's two doors, actually. From the back parking lot. Both of them are painted black. One has white letters on it that say Exit Only. The other has yellow letters on it that say Enter Here. You go in there. Through the entryway. Through a second door. Down a long hall toward the front of the building. The Airline Highway side. Near the front of the building, that hallway turns to the left and you go into the room where the women come out and you choose one. This is embarrassing to talk about it this way. Right there where the hall turns, there's a big flower pot with a fake tree in it. But behind the plant there's a short hall that would take you to a door. The front door. If you could get past the fake tree. I hope that makes sense."

"Was this the first time you'd been to the tanning salon?"

"Yes. The only time I've been there."

"Was this a front door like you could use to enter the building?"

"Yes. Well ... I mean, no. You could it if was open, but it was locked."

"How do you know it was locked?"

"I saw it when I came in. As I came up the hall I could see past the flower pot. It had a chain and a padlock on it. There were double doors. Had a chain through the panic bars with a padlock."

Fifty-three

At lunch Scott returned to his office at the church. Eloise Pennington, the church secretary, stopped him in the hallway.

"You have a visitor."

Scott looked past her.

"Okay. I'll see them in a minute."

He started around her. Eloise touched his shoulder.

"Wait. You can't go in there yet."

Scott frowned at her.

"What's going on?"

"She's here."

"Who?"

"Her."

Scott stared at her, thinking. Suddenly he knew.

"She's here?"

"Yes."

"In my office?"

"Yes."

Scott threw up his hands in frustration.

"What were you thinking?"

"What was I supposed to do with her, turn her out on the street?"

Scott gestured for her to be quiet.

"Lower your voice."

"'Lower my voice.' You lower yours."

He took a deep breath.

"Okay." He bumped his fist against his chin as he thought. "Okay." He pointed a finger in the air. "This is what I want you to do. Is Mary here?"

"No. She doesn't come in until tomorrow."

"Good. Check in her office and see if there's any money in there."

Eloise looked askance.

"Okay."

"How much do you have on you?"

"About forty dollars."

Scott looked away, counting in his mind.

"Okay. I have fifty. What's in petty cash?"

"About three hundred."

Scott's face brightened.

"Great. Get the petty cash. Your money. Check in Mary's office and see what's in there."

He moved past her down the hall. As he turned to enter his office he glanced over his shoulder. Eloise was still standing right where he'd left her. He twirled a hand over his shoulder.

"Get moving."

Eloise started up the hall. Scott stepped into his office.

Fifty-four

At one o'clock Scott left the church and returned to Somerset's office. All the way there he tried to think of what he could say when Somerset asked him about Tatiana. He was sure that was coming soon. When he reached the conference room, he still hadn't come up with any way to respond except to refuse to answer. That, he was sure, would land him in jail. He paused long enough to take a bottle of water from the table by the door, then made his way to the chair at the end of the conference table.

Somerset flipped through the pages of his legal pad.

"I think you told me this before, but where is Raisa now?"

Scott leaned back in his chair.

"As far as I know, she is in Bosnia."

"Bosnia?"

"Yes."

"That's where she was from?"

"Yes."

"And she's back there now?"

"That's what she said."

"Did Raisa go with you when you took these women in the van to wherever it was you took them? Was she with you? Did she ride with you?"

"Yes. She rode with me."

"Did you talk to her? Either in the van on the way to wherever it was or while you were there. Did you talk to her? You've told us several things she said. Other than that. Did you talk to her alone?"

"Yes. I've already told you about that."

"What language did these women speak? Did they speak English?"

"Like I said before, they spoke English. But some of them didn't speak it very well. I'm not sure what their native language is. Russian maybe. I don't know. But Raisa was the most fluent in English."

"Raisa could speak English better than the other women?"

"Yes."

"What did you talk about?"

"Mostly about how they came to be in the United States."

"That's a good question. How did they come to be in the United States? What did she tell you about that?"

"She wanted to get into show business. There was—"

"How old is she?"

"She's probably midtwenties. Maybe late twenties. I don't think she's thirty yet."

"How old are the other women?"

"About the same age."

"Okay. She wanted to be an actress. Raisa. She was trying to get to the United States so she could pursue a career as an actress?"

"Yes. A man at an agency in Bosnia told her he could get her started."

"An agency?"

"Yes. Like a talent agency, I suppose."

"Did she give you this man's name?"

"No."

"So he sent her to the United States."

"He told her she should work locally, get some experience, then he could get her work in other places. Eventually get her into the entertainment business in America."

"And she believed him."

"Yes. I guess."

"What kind of education did she have?"

"I don't know. She didn't say. We didn't talk about that. She seemed like an intelligent person."

"And she believed this man."

"I suppose."

"All right. What next? What happened next?"

"She signed an agreement with him. He took her as a client for a percentage of what she made. Put her to work at a club in Banja Luka."

"That's a city?"

"Yes."

"In Bosnia?"

"Yes."

"Spell it."

"B-A-N-J-A L-U-K-A. Two words."

"What was she doing there? At this club. Waiting tables? Stripping?"

"Dancing."

"Stripping."

"Not at first. This wasn't a strip club. The first place there in Banja Luka. They had a band. Several singers. A couple of dance troupes. I think they actually put on shows. After a month or two he sent her to a club in Mostar."

"Spell it."

"M-O-S-T-A-R."

"Still in Bosnia?"

"Yes. They had some entertainment there at this second place, but she was sent there to perform in the nude. They told her it was part of her training."

"Training for what?"

"They told her that all American actresses have to perform scenes in the nude. That she might as well get used to it this way."

"And she believed them."

"Well, there is a lot of nudity in American films."

"In *The Matrix*?"

"No. Not in *The Matrix*."

"Okay. She was in the club at Mostar. Then what?"

"After she'd been there a few months, a man showed up. Said he liked the way she worked, wanted to hire her for his club. She agreed. He took her to Italy. Gave her a job at a club in Turin."

"This man who hired her away from the club in Mostar. Was he from Italy?"

"I don't know."

"The first guy. In Bosnia. Did he own the club where she worked?"

"I don't know. I don't know anything about it. I'm just telling you what she told me."

"What about this second guy? In Italy. Did he own the club in

Italy where she worked?"

"She never said. I don't know."

"Okay. She was in Italy."

"Right. This place in Turin was a strip club. Actually the way she described it made it sound more like a brothel with a dance hall."

"What happened there? What did she do there?"

"She danced, at first. As a stripper. Then they told her she had to work as a prostitute."

"Did she?"

"Not at first. She tried to leave."

"Did they try to stop her?"

"They told her she could leave if she paid what she owed. That's when she found out the first guy, the one from Bosnia, had actually sold her to the guy from Italy."

"He sold her?"

"Yes."

"How did he do that?"

"The first guy. The guy she signed with originally. He said she owed him for training, costumes, clothes. Kind of a company store deal. The guy from Italy paid him and then said Raisa owed him for that, plus a few more things."

"What did she do?"

"She didn't have the money. She tried to leave anyway. They beat her. Raped her. Forced her to dance and ... whatever."

"They forced her to do ... to be a prostitute?"

"Yes. Made a couple of porn films."

"In Italy?"

"Yes. And later here in Mobile. According to what she said."

"She performed in porn films here? In Mobile?"

"Yes."

"Where? Where were these films made?"

"Some motel. Best I could tell from what she said, it was some-where out on Highway 90."

"Did she know the name?"

"No."

"Did she tell you anything about making any movies at the tan-ning salon?"

"No."

"Did she tell you anything about making any movies at the warehouse?"

"No."

"Did she tell you about performing any... doing any ... Did she tell you about any sexual activity taking place at the warehouse?"

"Yes."

"What did she say took place there?"

"She said there was one customer who came there a few times."

"To the warehouse? He came to the warehouse?"

"Yes."

"Who was it?"

"She didn't know his name."

"Anyone else come there? To the warehouse."

"She didn't tell me about anyone else."

"Okay. She went to this club in Italy. Turin, Italy. Then what?"

"From there she was sent to Mexico City."

"What happened there?"

"Not much. She worked a few weeks at a club. But she wasn't there long. Then they brought her to Texas with a group of other women. Most of them were from Croatia."

"Had she been with these other women before? Was this the first time she saw them?"

"I think this was the first time she saw them. I understood her to say she came from Italy by herself. I mean, there weren't any other women with her. Someone was with her on the trip."

"How did they travel? Plane? Boat?"

"They came on a freighter. A freight ship."

"From Italy to Mexico?"

"Yes."

"Okay. She was in Mexico. She came to Texas. What happened in Texas?"

"She was in Dallas for a few days. Then to New Orleans. Then to Mobile."

"Did she work anywhere in Dallas?"

"No. Not that she told me."

"Did she tell you about working in New Orleans?"

"No."

"She told you all of this herself? What you've been telling me about Bosnia, to Italy, to Mexico, to the U.S. She told you all of that herself?"

"Yes."

"Did the entire group she was with in Mexico ... The group they brought over to Texas. Did they all come to Mobile?"

"I don't know."

"Were all the women at the tanning salon also women who came with her from Mexico?"

"I don't know. You'd have to ask her."

"I would love to ask her, but I can't. So I have to ask you."

"If she said, I don't remember. But I don't think she said."

"Why is she back in Bosnia?"

"You should ask someone else about that."

"Are you saying you don't know?"

"I'm saying, you've asked me this two or three times. I've told you all I know about it."

"Did she mention any of these men? The one in Bosnia. The one in Italy. Mexico. Texas. New Orleans. Mobile. Did Raisa mention any of the people she dealt with in those places by name?"

"No."

"Texas, New Orleans, Mobile. She didn't call anyone by name in any of those places?"

"She mentioned Manny Fernandez. Pete Rizutto. She talked a lot about a guy who was Rizutto's driver, but she didn't mention him by name."

"What did she say about them? About Fernandez and Rizutto?"

"She said Manny Fernandez managed the tanning salon. Mr. Rizutto owned it."

"She said Mr. Rizutto owned the salon?"

"Yes."

"What about the motel where the films were made? Did she say who owned that?"

"No. Just that it was another part of Rizutto's business."

"He was the one making the films?"

"Yes. Now I don't know any of this for myself. I'm just telling you what she told me."

Fifty-five

Glover was waiting by Hayford's car as Hayford came from the deposition. He rushed forward as Hayford came in sight.

"She's here."

Hayford glanced around, checking to see who might be watching, then pulled Glover aside.

"You're sure?"

"Yeah. I had a couple of guys at the bus station. One of them saw her earlier today."

"How early?"

"I don't know. I think it was sometime before lunch."

Hayford bellowed.

"Before lunch? What do you mean before lunch? That was five hours ago and you're just telling me now?"

Glover gestured with his hand.

"Calm down. They tried to call, but their cell phone was dead. So they followed her."

Hayford was still upset.

"The cell phone was dead? What kind of a job is this?"

"These are friends of mine. They aren't professionals, okay? They did the best they could."

Hayford took a deep breath and tried to get control of himself.

"Okay." He ran his fingers through his hair. "They saw her. They followed her. Where'd she go?"

Glover grinned.

"The church."

Hayford turned to the car.

"Get in."

Minutes later they rounded the corner onto Church Street.

St. Pachomius Church sat in the middle of the next block. Glover pointed.

"There they are."

Two young men sat on the front steps of the church. Hayford brought the car to a stop at the base of the steps. He threw open the door and jumped out.

"Where is she?"

The young men stood.

"She went inside. She hasn't come out yet."

Hayford stared at them for a moment, then looked at Glover.

"This place have a back door?"

They jumped in Hayford's car and made the block around the church. As they turned the corner, the rear entrance came into sight. The windows were dark. There wasn't a car in sight.

Hayford shouted.

"No!" He pounded the dash with his fist. "No. No. No."

He jerked his head toward Glover, his hands flailing the air.

"Tell me this didn't happen."

Glover looked away.

Fifty-six

*I*t was eight o'clock that night when Scott turned the car into the parking lot at the Oyster House, a restaurant on the causeway east of town. He drove around the side of the building. Eloise's car was already there. He backed the car into the spot next to hers and lowered the window.

"Everything go all right?"

"Yeah."

"You gave her the money?"

Eloise nodded.

"I gave her the money."

"Have you been back to the office?"

Eloise glared at him.

"No. I haven't been back to the office. You think I'm crazy?"

"Take tomorrow off."

"I don't think so."

"Why not?"

"If someone's watching and I'm not there, they'll know something's up."

Scott grinned.

"Okay. Did you get the phones?"

"Yes."

Eloise picked up a cell phone from the seat beside her and handed it through the window to him.

"Here. I got one for you too."

"Great. Where'd you get them?"

"Wal-Mart. Just outside Pensacola. Stopped on the way over."

Scott smiled.

"Had Tatiana ever been to a Wal-Mart?"

Eloise grinned.

"It was consumer overload."

Scott laughed.

"How many minutes did you get on her phone?"

"There's a hundred twenty minutes on both of them. We can add more to them online. I checked into it when I bought them."

"Do you know where she was going?"

"You told me not to find out."

"Did you find out?"

"No. I told her to get a ticket for the first bus going north. She went to the counter and got it herself. She wanted to tell me, but I stopped her."

"Did you see her get on the bus?"

Eloise nodded.

"It left a few minutes after we got there. I waited until she was on, watched her get in. Saw it when it left the parking lot."

"And you didn't look at the sign on the front that said where it was going?"

She shook her head.

"I did not."

"Okay." Scott reached to put the car in gear. "If you come in tomorrow, take that check to the bank and get the money for petty cash."

"What are you going to tell Mary?"

"I'm not going to tell Mary anything right now. And don't you, either."

Eloise frowned.

"She'll want to know."

"If she asks, tell her to deposit the check I put on her desk and I'll fill her in later."

He looked her in the eye.

"Thanks, Eloise."

Eloise nodded.

"You owe me."

Fifty-seven

*T*he following morning Scott lingered at the altar after morning prayers. When everyone was gone, he took a seat on the kneeling pad and leaned against the altar rail. Around him morning light poured through the stained-glass windows. He let his eyes rove over them, thinking about the story depicted on each one. Before long, his mind was thousands of years away, and the things that had seemed so heavy and troublesome when he'd awakened faded into the background.

By the time he reached Somerset's office, the peace he'd found in the nave had given way to a restless sense of urgency. He needed to get this deposition finished. He didn't need to be tied up another week with lawyers and questions about people and things that didn't matter.

Everyone was seated and waiting as he came down the hall.

"Let them wait," he mumbled. "If my life can wait, theirs can too."

He stopped at the table by the door and filled a cup with coffee, then made his way around the conference table and took a seat. The court reporter took a flash drive from her briefcase and plugged it into the dictation machine. Somerset took a sip of coffee. Scott moved forward in the chair and propped his elbows on the table.

"I've been here so long, I'm starting to remember what it was like to be a lawyer."

"Do you miss it?"

Scott shook his head.

"Not one bit, but my parishioners are starting to notice I'm not in the office."

Somerset took another sip of coffee.

"Well, there shouldn't be too much more to go, I think."

Scott nodded.

"That's what you said two days ago."

The men around the table chuckled. Somerset didn't respond. Scott managed a smile.

"I don't think I know much more."

Somerset took one more sip of coffee and nodded to the court reporter.

"We'll see about that." He took a document from beneath the legal pad, glanced at it, then looked over at Scott. "You were telling me earlier about the Saturday you went to the tanning salon, and I don't think we finished with that. You went there. The women came out. Pick it up from there. You chose Raisa. Then what?"

Scott sighed and leaned away from the table.

"She led me down a hallway to a room. We went inside. She closed the door. She asked me what I wanted. I told her a dance. She told me the price."

"A dance? What kind of dance?"

"I don't know."

"Well, you asked for it. What were you asking for?"

"I don't know. Mike said to ask her to dance. She would know what to do. I asked her to dance. She said it was a hundred dollars. I paid her. She started dancing."

"You paid her a hundred dollars?"

"Yes."

"In cash?"

"Yes."

"To dance."

"To dance."

"Then what?"

"She started dancing."

"Dancing?"

"Yes."

"There was music in there?"

"Yes."

"Were you dancing with her?"

"No."

"What were you doing?"

"Sitting in a chair."

"Okay. She started dancing. Then what?"

"Then she started taking off her clothes."

"What happened next?"

"I stared at the floor."

"You stared at the floor."

"Yes."

"And then what?"

"Waited for her to finish."

"You didn't peek?"

"No."

The answer made Scott uncomfortable. It wasn't exactly correct, but he'd sat there in that chair for days, answering question after question about things that had nothing to do with the case Somerset was supposed to be defending, and he was angry.

Somerset looked skeptical.

"Not just a little bit?"

"Not just a little bit."

"So you just sat there with your head down?"

"After a minute or two, I closed my eyes." He knew that part was true. He had closed his eyes. "I tipped my head down, closed my eyes, and whispered the message to her."

"Why not just tell her straight out?"

"Mike told me they probably taped whatever happened in the room. I didn't want them to see me in there and know what I was doing. Ruin the whole thing."

"She could hear you over the music?"

"Yes. It wasn't that loud. Plays all the time but it wasn't that loud. She was just a few feet away."

"Okay. You sat there with your eyes closed until she was finished."

"Yes."

"Then what?"

"She put her clothes on. Opened the door. I walked out. She disappeared."

"If your eyes were closed, how did you know she was naked?"

"Before I closed my eyes—when I was sitting there staring at the floor—I saw her clothes hit the floor near my feet."

"And you didn't peek just a little bit."

"Well ..." Scott blushed. This was the one thing he'd wanted to avoid. "I caught a glimpse of her as I ducked my head." To his surprise, no one in the room laughed. He had an embarrassed smile. "That's why I ducked my head."

"Have you seen a tape of what happened in that room?"

Scott's eyes were wide.

"They really made one?"

"Have you seen one?"

"No. Did they make a tape?"

"Has anyone told you a tape actually exists?"

"No. Does it?"

"After you delivered the message, what happened next?"

"I left. Drove home. Is there a tape?"

Somerset ignored him.

"What did you do next?"

"Took a shower. Went to bed."

"The next day would have been ..."

"Sunday."

Somerset nodded.

"Yes. Sunday. You went to church."

"Went to church."

"What time? What time did you get to church?"

"First service is at eight. We get together to pray around seven. Have the service at eight. Then another at ten thirty."

"Did you talk to anyone that Sunday about what you had done the night before?"

"No."

"Did anyone talk to you? Ask you about it? Say they saw you there?"

"No."

"Did you preach the sermon that Sunday?"

"Yes."

"What did you preach about?"

"The hidden things will be brought to light. Whatever you do in secret will be shouted from the mountaintop."

Somerset arched an eyebrow.

"Interesting. You remember that sermon, or did you check someplace before you came here today?"

"I remember it."

"Did you prepare for this deposition?"

"What do you mean?"

"Did you review any notes? Talk to anyone? That sort of thing?"

"No."

"Did you talk to Mike Connolly about this deposition?"

"You asked me that before. I told him about receiving the subpoena."

"What did he say?"

"He said I should tell the truth."

Fifty-eight

*T*atiana opened her eyes and surveyed the motel room. The furniture was worn and scratched. The carpet on the floor was threadbare, and the sheets on the bed were so thin she could see straight through them, but for thirty-five dollars a night she didn't complain. Besides, she had one thing there she hadn't enjoyed in a long time—freedom. She rolled on her side and checked the clock on the nightstand. It was eleven twenty-five.

As a child growing up in Bosnia, she'd first heard of Nashville when a friend of a friend let her listen to an Alan Jackson tape. Since then she'd often wondered what it was like in a city that made that kind of music. When Eloise told her to pick a destination, Tatiana thought of Nashville.

A few minutes later she climbed from the bed and walked to the window. She pushed aside the curtain and peeked out at an empty parking lot and the tall buildings beyond. Across the parking lot was a Waffle House. Her stomach growled. She turned toward the shower.

Fifty-nine

As the afternoon rolled on, Scott was certain that Somerset would ask about Tatiana—if he'd seen her, where she was, what had happened to her. There wasn't much more for them to discuss.

"Okay. You went to the tanning salon Saturday evening. Went to church Sunday morning. Church let out. What then?"

"Lunch. Nap. Couple of phone calls. Nothing to do with any of this."

"Did you have lunch at home?"

"No. We usually go out."

"Where did you go that Sunday?"

"I'm not sure. Probably A Spot of Tea."

"On Dauphin Street?"

"Yes."

"See anyone you knew?"

"I'm sure I did. Many of our church members go there for lunch. But I don't remember anyone in particular that day."

"All right. You had lunch. Went home. Placed a few ... Did you go straight home after lunch?"

"I don't remember anything about that afternoon. I mean, nothing stands out in my mind. Went to church. Went to lunch. Went home. Made a phone call or two. Took a nap. Then Mike Connolly came by."

"You remember making some phone calls that specific day? The Sunday after the Saturday when you went to the tanning salon?"

"Yes."

"Why do you remember those calls?"

"One was from the lady who cares for my father. There was a

little bit of a problem with him. The other was a call to my daughter."

"And why do you remember the call to your daughter?"

"She's my daughter."

"Now, Saturday night. After you were at the tanning salon. The women got out of the warehouse. What do you know about that?"

"They ... I wasn't there. All I know is just what I heard."

"From whom?"

"From Hollis and Mike. From hearing the women talk. Overhearing what was said."

"Okay. What did they say?"

"They said Mike and Hollis went to the warehouse that night. Picked up the women. Took them to Mrs. Gordon's house. They stayed there that night. Then the next day—"

"They? Who stayed there?"

"The women."

"Did Hollis Toombs or Mr. Connolly spend the night there? At Mrs. Gordon's."

"I don't know."

"Okay. The next day. That would be Sunday?"

"Yes."

"What happened that day? Sunday. After church. Pick up where you left off. You talked to the lady about your father. Then you called your daughter. Then what?"

"Mike came to my house late that afternoon. Asked me if—"

"How late?"

"I don't remember the time. It was getting dark."

"Okay. Then what?"

"He asked me if I would drive the women to this other location in the church van."

"So he told you they were out of the warehouse?"

"Yes. They got them out. Would I drive them someplace."

"And you said yes?"

"I said I would."

"At that point how many people knew where the women were?"

"I don't know. At that point I didn't know where they were."

"He didn't tell you?"

"No. He just asked me if I would drive them. I said yes. He told me to get the van gassed up and he'd call me and tell me where to meet him."

"Did he call you?"

"Yes."

"Where was he when he placed the call?"

"I don't know."

"Was it a cell phone? Was he calling from a cell phone?"

"Yes. He called me from his cell phone."

"And where were you?"

"I think I was in the van by then."

"So he called to you on your cell phone?"

"Yes."

"And where did he tell you to pick them up?"

"He told me to meet him at Mrs. Gordon's house."

"Had you ever been to her house before?"

"No. He told me how to get there."

"And where is that house located?"

"Houston Street."

"Did you go straight there?"

"Yes. I was leaving the gas station when he called. I went right on over there."

"What gas station were you at?"

"Chevron on Government Street."

"You bought gas there?"

"Yes. I filled up the van."

"Who paid for it?"

"I did."

"You, personally?"

"Yes."

"Did you get a receipt?"

"No."

"Did you pay with a credit card?"

"No. I paid cash."

"Any particular reason why you paid with cash?"

"I wasn't sure what was going to happen. If something went wrong, I didn't want to have a receipt."

"What did you think might go wrong?"

"I had no idea. I just didn't want to use my credit card for it."

"You drove to Mrs. Gordon's house. Then what?"

"I pulled up in front of the house. Mike was there. Hollis was there. Soon as I got there, they started loading up."

"They were waiting on you?"

"Yes. They were ready to go. Didn't take ten minutes to get everyone loaded."

"And you said Mrs. Gordon went with you?"

"She followed in her car. Took two of the women with her and followed in her car."

"How did you know where you were going with these women?"

"Mike told me the general area when he came by the house."

"And where was that?"

"Cape San Blas."

"In Florida?"

"Yes."

"How did you know where the house was? The particular house you went to. How did you know where it was?"

"Hollis knew. He told me how to get there."

"Had Hollis been there before?"

"No. I don't think so. He didn't act like it."

"And you had never been there before?"

"No."

"Mr. Connolly gave Hollis directions to the house?"

"Yes."

"Mr. Connolly had been there before?"

"Yes."

"This house was owned by Mr. Connolly's brother?"

"Yes. Rick."

"Have you ever met Rick? Did I ask you that before?"

"I don't remember if you asked me. But, no, I've never met him."

"He didn't come down when Mr. Connolly was going through withdrawal?"

"No. That's why Mrs. Gordon called me. The landlord called Rick. Rick called Mrs. Gordon. Mrs. Gordon called me."

"She called you while Mr. Connolly was going through this detox?"

"Yes."

"Were you present when Mr. Connolly gave Hollis Toombs directions to the house?"

"No."

"Then how do you know he did?"

"He told me. Just before we left. We were all in the van. Ready to go. Hollis got in. Mike leaned through the window and told me Hollis knew where we were going."

"Did Hollis ride with you all the way to the house?"

"Yes."

"Did you stop anywhere along the way?"

"We stopped at McDonald's to eat."

"Where?"

"In Panama City."

"Mrs. Gordon stopped there too?"

"Yes."

"Why did she go?"

"I think she didn't like the idea of all those women being over there with two men."

"Was that a problem?"

"No. She just didn't like it."

"What time did you leave from her house?"

"Late that afternoon. Early that evening. It was after dark when we left, I think. But it wasn't very late."

"You drove the van?"

"Yes."

Sixty

*L*ate that night Scott was awakened by the ring of the cell phone. He reached for the lamp on the nightstand and knocked the clock to the floor.

Maggie groaned.

"What are you doing?"

"I'm trying to find the phone."

He swung his feet from beneath the covers and sat on the edge of the bed. The cell phone lay on the floor by his shoes. He picked it up and pressed a button to answer the call.

Tatiana's voice was unmistakable.

"I hope I didn't wake you."

"Is everything all right?"

"Yes. I'm in—"

He cut her off.

"Don't tell me where you are."

"You don't want to know?"

"I would love to know, but someone else might hear us."

"Oh. Okay."

"I want you to pick a location somewhere else in the country. A city you've always wanted to see."

"Some other city than this one?"

"Yes."

"Okay."

"And I want you to go to that city."

"Go to some other city?"

"Yes. Pick some city in America you've wanted to see. And go there. When you get there, give me a call."

"Is everything okay?"

"Yes. Everything is okay. You'll be safe as long as you don't stay anywhere very long."

"Okay. Pick a new city and go there."

"Yes. And call me when you get there. At this number."

"At your house?"

"No. No. Not at my house. Call the cell phone number."

Maggie rolled over to face him.

"The same number she just called."

Scott nodded.

"Call me at the same number you called tonight."

"Two five one, four—"

Scott cut her off again.

"No. Don't say the number. Just call me at that number when you get where you're going."

"Okay."

Scott pressed a button to end the call and laid the phone on the nightstand. He fell back in bed and lay there, staring up at the ceiling.

Maggie rolled against his side and slipped her arm across his chest.

"Think she'll be all right?"

"She'll be fine, as long as I don't mess up the answers to Somerset's questions."

"How many ways can he ask you about what happened?"

"I don't know, but he's doing his best to find them all."

Sixty-one

On the way downtown the next morning Scott thought about his conversation with Tatiana the night before. Once again his mind turned to how he would answer the questions about her that he knew were coming. By the time he reached Broad Street he had worried himself into a tense and irritable mood. He parked on Dauphin Street and started down the sidewalk.

The conference room was full when he arrived. Everyone was seated and waiting. Somerset looked up as Scott moved toward his chair.

"Anytime you feel like dropping by, just come on in."

Scott glared at him.

"You said this would be finished three days ago."

Somerset smiled.

"Not too much more."

Scott took a seat. Somerset glanced over at the court reporter. She nodded. Somerset began.

"You mentioned before about Steve Ingram and referred to his father as Joe Ingram. Do you know Mr. Ingram?"

"Yes."

The question caught Scott off guard. Not because it raised a sensitive issue, but because it was so unrelated to the questions he had been asked the day before.

Somerset kept going.

"How do you know Joe Ingram?"

"His father and my father were friends."

"Your father had a lot of friends."

"It was a rural county. He practiced law in the county seat. Not much there but pine trees. There weren't many lawyers back then.

Very few in the southern end of the state."

"So how was it your father came to know Joe Ingram's father?"

"Timber."

"Timber?"

"Mr. Ingram, the father, Joe Ingram's father, was in the timber business. I mean, he owned the shipyard, but he owned a lot of timberland too. My grandfather was well known in the area and very well known among timber people. My father followed in his steps. The two of them got to be acquainted."

"Over a stand of pine trees."

"Yes. Acres and acres of pine trees. That and hunting."

Scott began to relax. The tension eased from his body. Somerset's questions led him down a familiar path filled with memories of a time he remembered well.

"They enjoyed hunting?"

"Yes. Joe's father used to come up to see my father during hunting season. They met at The Pond. Hunted all day. Talked business all night."

"The Pond?'"

"That's what we call it. It's a hunting camp."

"And that's where you met Joe Ingram?"

"Yes. Dad would let me tag along. Mr. Ingram brought Joe. We became acquainted that way. I was a young boy. Probably ten or twelve. Joe was a good bit older. But when Mr. Ingram came up, we were the only ones in the camp. Just the four of us."

"Does your father have any siblings?"

"Yes. He had three sisters and a brother. The brother and two of the sisters are dead."

"And the third sister?"

"She lives in Wiggins. Wiggins, Mississippi. Down there in Stone County where they grew up."

"So you met Joe Ingram at your family hunting camp?"

"Yes."

"And you became friends."

"Yes. Of sorts. When they hunted birds, I carried the dead birds. When they hunted deer, I carried the gear and kept everyone's glass full. If we were up there during dove season, I shucked the oysters."

"Oysters?"

"Mr. Ingram. Not Joe. His father. The old man. He loved raw oysters. When we had a dove hunt he'd bring a sack of them up there. They'd carry an ice chest or a gunny sack full of them out to the field. Mr. Ingram sat on a stool and shot birds. I sat beside him and shucked oysters in between fetching the dead birds."

"Never heard of such a thing."

"It's a lifestyle that's pretty much disappeared."

"I reckon so. Did you know his sons? Joe Ingram. Did you know Joe Ingram's sons?"

"I think I met all of them. As I recall, there were three. Frank. I told you about meeting him. Steve. I think I met him. I'm not sure. And then the youngest. Joey. He comes to our church occasionally."

"Do you know Joe Ingram's wife?"

"I've met her. That's about it."

Sixty-two

*T*hat same morning Castille arrived at the airport in Orlando, Florida. He made his way past baggage claim and stepped outside. A man met him there and led him toward a car parked nearby. Castille got in on the passenger side.

"You found both of them?"

The man steered the car into traffic.

"Yeah. First call came from a cell phone registered to Catherine Hanks. Lives in Pine Hills."

"You know the address?"

"Yeah. We got somebody watching the house."

He checked the mirror and changed lanes. Castille flipped open his cell phone. He talked while he scrolled through a list of missed calls and voice mails.

"Did you try to talk to her?"

"No. You said for us to wait."

"Is she home now?"

"She was when I left."

Castille closed the phone and looked up.

"Take me over there."

Sixty-three

*S*cott sighed and crossed his legs. Somerset took a sip of coffee.

"Okay. I want to ask you a few questions about something else. Mr. Connolly lives in a guesthouse in midtown."

"Yes."

"Before he lived in that guesthouse, he lived in an apartment. Carondolet Apartments."

"They were on Carondolet. I don't know if that was the name of them."

"Did you ever visit him in that apartment?"

"Just the time I went over there when he was coming off alcohol."

"When Mrs. Gordon called you?"

"Yes."

"Straighten me out on this. Earlier, when I asked you about whether you'd ever been to his house, I understood you to say you'd never been there. Then you told me about going to the guesthouse two or three times. Now you're telling me about a visit to the apartment?"

"I'm sorry. Yes. I went to the apartment."

"How did that happen?"

"The landlord called Mr. Connolly's brother, Rick. Rick called Mrs. Gordon. Mrs. Gordon called me. I went over to his apartment."

"Who else was there?"

"Mrs. Gordon. Barbara."

"Barbara?"

"His ex-wife."

"His ex-wife was there?"

"Yes."

"Is that all? Anybody else there?"

"While I was there, no. That's all who were there."

"What did you do?"

"Helped Mrs. Gordon get him in the shower."

"Okay. Anything else?"

"Helped her make the bed. While I had him in the shower, she and Barbara changed the sheets. I got him back to the bed and helped them finish up."

"Do anything else?"

"No. I don't think so. I was mostly just there."

"Why did he move from that apartment to the guesthouse?"

"It burned."

"The apartment burned?"

"Yes."

"Did you and Mr. Connolly ever talk about that?"

"About the apartment?"

"Yes. Did you and Mr. Connolly ever talk about Mr. Connolly's apartment burning?"

"Once."

"Tell me about that conversation."

"He came by the church one day. After that. After the apartment burned and he'd moved to the guesthouse. I asked him if—"

"Did he go immediately to the guesthouse?"

"No. He went to the hospital. Then he lived at the Admiral Semmes Hotel for a week or two."

"How long was he in the hospital?"

"Not long. Not even overnight, I don't think. Just long enough for them to check him out. Make sure he was okay."

"He was there when the apartment burned?"

"He told me he unlocked the door and the place blew up in his face. Knocked him across the hallway outside his apartment. Next thing he knew he was laying on a stretcher behind an ambulance."

"Okay. He came by the church. You were talking about it."

"Yeah. I asked him if they'd found out what happened. You know, who did it. He said he knew who did it but he wasn't talking."

"He said he knew who blew up his apartment?"

"Yes."

"Did he ever tell you?"

"No."

"Was this before or after the time he talked to you about what he said happened in the hangar?"

"This was after. After the hangar. Judge Agostino had been arrested and the news had died down about that. It had been a month or so. The conversation ... We were talking a month or so after all of that."

"Is that it? Did he say any more about it?"

"Told me it was a total loss. He lost everything in the apartment."

Sixty-four

*C*astille stepped from the car and scanned the street. To the left a car was parked two houses up the street. Across from it was a pickup parked in the wrong direction. To the right a white van was parked in the next block with two tires on top of the curb. On the side of the van was a logo for a cable company. Somewhere behind him Castille heard a dog bark. A breeze rustled through the trees. He listened to hear behind the noise, then started toward the house.

Made of concrete blocks, the house was a single-story structure. From the way it looked, it had been constructed sometime in the 1950s. A driveway led from the street to a carport on the side. There was a Buick LeSabre parked there.

Castille made his way up the front steps and knocked on the door.

The door opened a little way and a woman peered out. She was dressed in loose-fitting blue jeans and a red blouse. She stood with one foot behind the door and held the knob in her hand.

Castille smiled at her.

"Hello. My name is Terry Cline. I'm a criminologist for the Orlando Police Department." He handed her a business card. "We're looking for a woman ..." He took a photo from his pocket and handed it to her. "This woman. We think you may have seen her."

Catherine looked at the photo.

"Is she in some kind of trouble?"

"She's an illegal. Working the streets."

Catherine frowned.

"Working the streets?"

Castille gave her a sheepish grin.

"Yes, ma'am. A hooker."

She handed the photo back to him.

"Yes. I've seen her."

"When?"

"I let her use my cell phone. I think it was night before last."

"Where were you?"

"Over on Colonial Drive."

"Where on Colonial?"

"The Krystal."

"What time was it?"

"I don't remember. Not too late. I don't stay out very late anymore. Stopped in there for a hamburger."

Castille smiled.

"Just one?"

She grinned.

"Well, I don't think anyone eats just one Krystal hamburger. I think I had three."

"She was in the store?"

"Yes. She was sitting at a booth. I sat at a table near her. My sister called me. I guess that's how she knew I had a phone. When I hung up from talking to my sister, she came over to the table and asked if she could use my phone."

"Is that all she said?"

"She said thank you."

"Notice anything else?"

"No. Pretty lady. A little ... She wasn't really dirty but she wasn't made up either. Had a foreign accent." Catherine looked up. "You sure she's the woman you're looking for?"

"Yes, ma'am," Castille replied. "She's the one."

"She seemed like a nice lady."

"They always do. Did she place a call?"

"She tried, but I don't think anyone answered. She didn't talk to anyone."

"Was she standing there with you the whole time?"

"Yes. She dialed the number and then looked very frustrated. She just ended the call and handed the phone back to me."

"That's it?"

"Yes."

"Was she still there when you left?"

"No. She handed me the phone and walked out. I saw her cross the parking lot in front of the Krystal and start down Colonial."

Castille backed away from the door.

"Thank you, ma'am. If she tries to contact you again, I'd appreciate a call."

Castille started toward the car. Catherine closed the door.

Sixty-five

*S*omerset took a photograph from his file and slid it across the table toward Scott.

"I've marked this photograph as defendant Buie Hayford's Exhibit Number One to your deposition. Describe that photograph, please."

Scott glanced at the photo.

"It's a picture of a man. Looks like he's at a country club. He's standing beside a golf cart."

"Let the record reflect the witness has correctly described the picture."

Larry King spoke up.

"Object to the form of the question."

Somerset's forehead wrinkled in a frown.

"What question?"

King pointed to the photograph.

"The picture stands for itself. The jury can decide on its own whether he described the picture or not."

"I just want the record to be clear."

"You marked it. She's got it on the list. The record speaks for itself."

Somerset picked up the photograph and held it for Scott to see.

"Father Scott, do you recognize the man in this picture? Defendant's Exhibit One to your deposition?"

"Just from seeing him in the newspaper."

"When was that? When did you see his picture in the newspaper?"

"I don't remember the date."

"That was in the *Press-Register*?"

"Yes."

"See anything about him in any other newspapers?"

"No."

"Do you know him?"

"No."

"His name is Ford Defuniak. I asked you about him before. Does that name mean anything to you?"

"No."

"He worked in the trust department at Tidewater Bank. I think I mentioned him to you before, but I want to make sure. You've remembered some things as we've gone along. Any of that ring a bell?"

"We have one member. Former member. Left a rather large estate. It's in a trust that's managed by Tidewater Bank. The church doesn't have anything to do with it except that every May we receive a gift from the trust for our summer Bible school program. That's the only thing I remember about their trust department."

"You said before that your church didn't do any business with Tidewater."

"We don't. We don't have any accounts with them. No investments with them. But after you asked me that, I remembered this estate gives us a gift every spring."

"What is the name of that estate?"

"Tankersly. Edna Tankersly."

"Is that the only time this trust makes a gift to the church?"

"Yes. She was a Sunday-school teacher. Enjoyed working with children. When she died, she had some great-grandchildren who were at our church. She wanted to make sure they had a program to attend so she included a gift to the church for it. The lawyer who prepared the trust document made a mistake. He was supposed to make the gift run until the youngest of her grandchildren came of age, but he didn't do it. He wrote it as a perpetual gift. At least for the life of the trust."

"And no one challenged it?"

"I don't guess. She found out about the problem before she signed the trust documents. He told her about it. She told him to just leave it like it was."

"When did she die?"

"I don't know. She had been dead a long time when I came here."

"How did you find out about that story?"

"Her son told me."

"What's his name?"

"Clark. Clark Tankersly."

"Do you know anyone who works in the trust department at Tidewater Bank?"

"No."

"Know anyone at the—"

"Yes."

"I need to finish the question before you answer."

"You asked me if I knew anyone at the bank. I know someone who works for Tidewater, but not in the trust department."

"Who?"

"Marie Ross. She works in the Irvington branch."

"Okay. What does she do there?"

"I think she's the branch manager."

"Anyone else at Tidewater Bank you know?"

"Not that I can recall."

"Know anyone else who works at the bank at all? Anywhere. Teller? Janitor? Anyone."

"No."

Sixty-six

Castille stared out the window at the Krystal restaurant.

"Go around the building one more time."

The man turned the car from the street into the drive-thru lane and slowly circled the building. As they came around the other side, Castille glanced over at him.

"What else is around here?"

"Not much. Fast-food places."

A car horn sounded behind them. Castille turned to look over the seat. They turned left and started up Colonial Drive. As they crossed the intersection with Johnson Young Parkway, he pointed out the window.

"Bus station is down there."

Castille jerked his head around to see.

"Where?"

By then they were beyond the traffic light.

"Down there. On Young Parkway."

"Turn around. Let's have a look."

The man slowed the car and waited for oncoming traffic, then crossed the turn lane and drove back in the opposite direction. At the intersection they turned right. The bus station was in the middle of the block.

Castille turned to look at it as they drove past.

"Pull over. Let's get out."

Sixty-seven

*S*omerset took several photographs from his file.

"All right. We're back. Let me show you two more pictures. We'll mark them as Defense Exhibits Six and Seven." He tossed the photos on the table in front of Scott. "Ever see either of those two men?"

"No."

"Never?"

"Not as far as I can recall."

"Okay." He picked up the photographs from the table. "Mr. Connolly is divorced, is he not?"

"Yes."

"Do you know his ex-wife?"

"I've met her."

"Ever talk to her about Mr. Connolly?"

"No."

"Ever been to her house?"

"No."

"Ever hear him talk about her?"

"Yes."

"What did he say?"

"The usual kind of stuff."

"You mean, he was still interested in her, or was he bashing her?"

"He was still interested."

"Are they back together?"

"No. Not yet."

"Okay. Let me ask you about someone named Marisa. Do you know anyone by that name?"

"Mike had a girlfriend named Marisa. Actually, that was her stage name."

"Do you know her real name?"

"Linda. Linda something. I don't remember her last name."

"Do you know where she lives?"

"No."

"You said Marisa was her stage name. Does she perform somewhere?"

"Yes. If that's who you're talking about. If that's the Marisa you're asking about, she was a dancer at the Imperial Palace. I don't know if she's still there or not."

"The club on the state line?"

"Yes."

"She's a stripper?"

"Yes."

"Ever see her perform?"

"Have I ever seen her perform?"

"Yes."

"No."

"Ever been to the Imperial Palace?"

"No."

"How did you know her? Marisa."

"She was at the apartment when I went over there."

"When you went over there and helped Mrs. Gordon? When he was trying to get off booze?"

"Yes."

"You didn't tell me about her before."

"Sorry."

"What was that like?"

"Seeing her?"

"No. Mr. Connolly. Coming off alcohol. What was that like? For him."

"Not very pretty."

"He had a bad problem with it?"

"Yes."

"How much was he drinking a day?"

"About a quart a day."

"A quart?"

"Somebody like that stops drinking all at once, it can get ugly."

"And it did?"

"Yes."

"Did you already know Mrs. Gordon? Before you met Mr. Connolly?"

"Yes."

"How did you know her?"

"She attends our church. Comes to the eight o'clock service on Sunday."

"Ever been to her house?"

"Just that one time when I picked up the women."

"From the warehouse?"

"Yes. The women from the warehouse."

"How long were they at Mrs. Gordon's house? The women from the tanning salon. The warehouse. How long did they stay at her house?"

"From what I understand, they spent that Saturday night there. Then we drove them to the beach house that next day. Late Sunday afternoon."

"All right. Just a minute. I think we're almost finished." Somerset looked through his notes. "Now. You touched on this once or twice, and I'd like to go back to it and clear it up. I think you sort of slid this past us. Or tried to slide it past us. You said there—"

"I didn't try to slide anything past anyone."

Somerset glanced at a document in his file, then back to Scott.

"You said there were eleven women."

"Tried to slide what past you?"

"You said there were eleven women. You and Hollis took eleven women to Cape San Blas. Isn't that what you said?"

"Yes. As best I recall."

"You took eleven over to Cape San Blas."

"Yes."

"And you said Raisa went home to Bosnia."

"Yes."

"That would leave ten."

"Yes."

"And Victoria married Hollis."

"Yes."

"That leaves nine."

"Yes."

Somerset took a document from his file and handed it to Scott. "Take a look at this."

Scott scanned over the page.

"What is this?"

"This is a document we've obtained that indicates the State Department settled eight women from this group."

"Where did you get this?"

"That's not my question for you, Rev. Nolan. What I want to know from you is where is the other woman?"

"What other woman?"

"There were eight women resettled by the State Department. By your count and ours there should have been nine. Isn't there one more woman?"

"You'd have to ask someone else about that."

"I'm asking you."

"Maybe there wasn't. Maybe I was wrong."

"No. I think you were right. Where is she, Rev. Nolan?"

"I'm not saying there was another woman. And I'm not saying there wasn't."

"Well, I need you to say. Where is she?"

"Can't say."

"Can't? Or won't?"

"Doesn't matter. I'm not saying."

"Do you know where she is?"

"I can't answer your question."

"Were you romantically involved with her?"

"I have been faithful to my wife in every way."

"What was this woman's name?"

"I can't answer your question."

"Well, I think we both know where this will take us."

Sixty-eight

*T*hat night Scott and Maggie ate at the Bluegill, a restaurant on the causeway not far from where he'd met Eloise a few nights before. On the way home he reached across the seat and took Maggie's hand.

"Do you think these women came into our life for nothing?"

Maggie shook her head. He smiled over at her.

"Neither do I. So don't worry. This will all work out."

Maggie turned away.

"What's the worst they can do?"

"The court?'

"Yes."

"Put me in jail until I answer Somerset's questions."

She turned to look at him.

"Do you think she'll do that?"

"I don't know. Greg thinks she probably will."

"I thought he knew her."

"He does, but that won't change what she does with the case."

Maggie sighed.

"It just seems so heavy."

"We're dealing with dark forces."

"I don't ..."

The cell phone rang. Maggie let go of his hand. Scott picked up the phone and pressed a button to take the call.

"Don't tell me where you are."

Tatiana giggled.

"I remember."

"Are you in a new place?"

"Yes."

"Good. Stay there tonight and I'll call you in the morning."

"Okay."

"Put the phone on the charger tonight so it will work tomorrow."

"Okay."

"Do you have enough money?"

"Yes. I'm fine."

"Okay. I'll call you in the morning."

Scott switched off the phone and laid it on the seat. Maggie squeezed his hand.

"What happens tomorrow?"

"I have a meeting with Dave Brenner."

"Who's that?"

"FBI agent."

"What do they want?"

"I asked for the meeting. Mike set it up."

Sixty-nine

The following morning Scott conducted morning prayers. For a few minutes he lost himself in the liturgy. All else faded from his mind. Then as the service concluded and the final words of benediction slipped past his lips, Mike Connolly appeared in the center aisle. Beside him was a man dressed in a dark suit. Connolly caught Scott's eye and gestured toward the man. The man slipped quietly into the last row of pews. Connolly disappeared.

When the last of the parishioners had filed past on their way out, the man rose from the pew and started down the aisle. Scott came down the chancel steps to the nave floor. The man nodded.

"I'm Dave Brenner. Mike Connolly said you wanted to talk."

Brenner glanced at his watch. Scott moved to the front pew.

"Let's sit here."

Brenner glanced around.

"You sure no one can hear us?"

"It won't matter."

Brenner took a seat on the pew.

"Mike said this was—"

Scott nudged him.

"Scoot over."

Brenner slid down the pew. Scott took a seat.

"Mr. Brenner, I don't think you and I have ever met."

"No. We haven't." Brenner glanced at his watch again. "I have an appointment. What was it you wanted?"

"There is a woman. Her name is Tatiana Perovic. The FBI or the U.S. Marshals or somebody in the federal government has been protecting her. She's supposed to testify before a grand jury here in Mobile."

"Have you heard from her?"

"Yes."

"Where is she?"

"I don't know. But I can get in touch with her."

"Is she still willing to cooperate?"

"Yes. I think so."

Brenner took a scrap of paper from his pocket.

"How can I get in touch with her?"

"You can't." Scott smiled. "I can."

"What do you mean?"

"Something spooked her."

"There was a robbery."

"That would do it."

"She ran."

"I can imagine. Look, I'm probably going to jail by the end of the week."

"What for?"

"I'm in the middle of a deposition and they started asking questions about her and—"

"John Somerset."

"Yes."

"We tried to talk to him. Not very cooperative."

"The real problem is his client."

"Buie Hayford."

"You're familiar with the situation."

Brenner grimaced.

"Know all about it."

"I need you to tell me where she should wait for you."

"We need to know where she is."

Scott shook his head.

"Can't work like that. You tell me where you want to meet her, and I'll tell her where to be."

Brenner's shoulders sagged.

"I'll call you. We'll have to get something set up."

Scott stood. Brenner stepped into the aisle. Scott shook his hand.

"Don't wait too long."

Seventy

*T*hree days later Scott was back in Judge McKenzie's courtroom. Judge McKenzie seemed amused to find them there again.

"Well, here we are once again, gentlemen. You all couldn't work this out among yourselves?"

Somerset stood.

"No, Your Honor."

"All right. We are here today on defendant Buie Hayford's second motion to compel answers at the deposition of one Andrew Scott Nolan. Mr. Somerset, you may proceed."

"Very well. I think it might help if I brought us all up to speed on this. As the court is aware, I noticed the deposition of Andrew Scott Nolan, who is the rector at St. Pachomius Church. Rev. Nolan appeared for that deposition. At some point in that deposition he refused to answer questions about a fishing trip he had taken with Keyton Attaway. We filed a motion. Came over here. You heard testimony and argument, and ruled in our favor. We went back, resumed the deposition. We had a telephone conference with you about one other point and then got all the way down almost to the end. I was just cleaning up a couple of things that I still had a question about. And Rev. Nolan refused to answer my questions about a witness. He didn't assert a privilege. Didn't give a reason. Just refused to answer."

"I read your motion. This is a lawsuit against Tidewater Bank. Something about a family trust?"

"Yes, Your Honor. Tidewater managed the Tonsmeyer Family Trust. That trust owns a number of pieces of commercial property. One of those is a building on Airline Highway that was occupied at one time by Panama Tan. A tanning salon. Some women worked there who were allegedly prostitutes. The trust also owns several warehouses on the docks. Supposedly the women at the tanning salon were living in one of those warehouses."

"They had something to do with one of Mike Connolly's cases?"

"Yes, Your Honor. Camille Braxton, one of the beneficiaries of the trust, was murdered. Her husband was charged with it. Mike Connolly represented him. Perry Braxton. Mike Connolly represented Perry Braxton."

"So why are we here with Rev. Nolan instead of Mike Connolly?"

"I'm trying to find out what happened at those properties. The trust is suing the bank and Buie Hayford and a dozen other folks over the way the trust was managed. Part of their complaint centers around matters involving Ford Defuniak. He was the officer at the bank who managed this trust. He would know about these things, but Mr. Defuniak is dead. Mr. Connolly can't tell us anything. Rev. Nolan was there. He knows a lot of what happened."

Judge McKenzie glanced over at Scott.

"Rev. Nolan was at the warehouse? Or the tanning salon?"

Somerset replied.

"The tanning salon, Your Honor. It doesn't appear he was there for the supposed ... It doesn't appear he was there for what you might think, based on the allegations. But he was there. He helped Mr. Connolly with something that had to do with the murder case. But he's one of the few available witnesses who can talk about this. And the woman we were asking him about during his deposition is one of the last of those women at the salon who is still accessible."

"What happened to the others?"

"They were resettled in various places by the State Department."

"The State Department? The U.S. State Department?"

"Yes, Your Honor. They were all from Eastern European countries. If you believe the allegations, they were brought here under duress. It's my understanding the State Department granted them asylum."

"And you don't know where they are."

"No. Not the ones who were resettled. One of them returned to her home in Europe to assist the authorities over there. And one married a man who lives here. And this lady we were asking about is the only other one."

"So you were asking about a woman who worked at this tanning salon, and Rev. Nolan refused to answer."

"Yes, Your Honor."

Judge McKenzie turned to Scott.

"Rev. Nolan?"

Scott stood.

"Yes, Your Honor."

"Is Mr. Collins representing you on this motion?"

"No, Your Honor."

"Do you wish to represent yourself?"

"I suppose."

"Are you asserting that these matters are protected by the privilege we discussed earlier? The priest-penitent privilege?"

"Well, I ... I think it would be best if I didn't answer that, Your Honor."

"You understand, we're here today to decide whether you will answer or not. I'm the one who decides that issue."

"Yes, Your Honor."

"Rev. Nolan, I think you need counsel to represent you. I'm going to recess this hearing for a few minutes and let you see if you can contact Mr. Collins."

Somerset tried to interrupt.

"Your Honor, we—"

Judge McKenzie stood.

"We are in recess, Mr. Somerset. Whatever you have to say, you can say it when we find Mr. Collins."

Seventy-one

*T*wo hours later Scott returned to Judge McKenzie's courtroom accompanied by Greg Collins. Judge McKenzie took a seat on the bench and glanced around the room.

"Well, I see we have found Mr. Collins."

Collins stood.

"Yes, Your Honor."

"Mr. Collins, have you had an opportunity to consult with Rev. Nolan?"

"Yes, Your Honor."

"Are you prepared to go forward with this matter?"

"Your Honor, could we continue this case to another day? I have had all of five minutes to consult with my client on this matter and I—"

"Mr. Collins, we've all been here before on this case. Actually twice as I recall. Once in court and once on the phone. You were here for one of those hearings. I think you and your client understand where we are on this. Your client chose to show up here in my court today on this matter without counsel. And, while I think he needs counsel for this hearing, I'm not inclined to let that delay us."

Judge McKenzie turned to Somerset.

"Mr. Somerset, this is your motion. Go ahead."

Somerset stood.

"Your Honor, with your indulgence, I would like to pick up with the question where we left off with Rev. Nolan on the stand."

"Mr. Collins?"

"We have no objection, Your Honor."

"Very well. Rev. Nolan. Come on up and take a seat in the witness stand."

Scott came around the judge's bench to the witness stand.

"Raise your right hand. Do you swear or affirm that the testimony you are about to give will be the truth, the whole truth, and nothing but the truth?"

"I affirm."

"Have a seat. Mr. Somerset."

Somerset stood in front of Scott.

"Rev. Nolan, we've discussed these matters in your deposition. But just to get us going, you told us you and Hollis Toombs drove some women over to a beach house on Cape San Blas. Isn't that correct?"

"Yes."

"These were women who had been working at a local tanning salon."

"Yes."

"And they were here illegally."

"Yes."

"Where had they been living?"

"As far as I know, they had been living in a warehouse down near the docks."

"You didn't personally see them there?"

"No."

"How did you come to know about these women?"

"Mike Connolly told me about them."

"What did he tell you about them?"

"He told me they had been brought here to work at the tanning salon."

"Did he tell you what sort of work they did there?"

"He said they were prostitutes."

"And why were you and Mr. Connolly talking about them?"

"He wanted me to help him get them out of the warehouse."

"Did you help him?"

"Yes."

"What did you do?"

"I went to the salon and delivered a message to one of the women there. And I drove them to a house in Florida."

"Where in Florida?"

"Cape San Blas."

"Whose house was it?"

"Rick Connolly's."

"Mike's brother?"

"Yes."

"Did you take these women over there by yourself?"

"No."

"Who went with you? Other than the women."

"A man named Hollis Toombs and Mike's secretary. Mrs. Gordon."

"Myrtice Gordon?"

"Yes."

"How many women did you take over there?"

"In total or in the van I drove?"

"In total."

"Eleven."

"Where are those women now?"

"Most of them have been resettled in various places, I think."

"You told me earlier one of those women returned to her home in Bosnia."

"Yes."

"One married Mr. Toombs. Hollis Toombs."

"Yes."

"That leaves nine."

Scott did not reply. Somerset retrieved a document from the counsel's table and handed it to Scott.

"Now I show you this document, which I showed you at your deposition. Do you remember that document?"

"I remember you showed it to me before."

"At your deposition I suggested to you that the State Department resettled eight of those women in the United States. You remember that?"

"That's what you said."

"And then I asked you what happened to the ninth woman."

"You said there was a ninth woman."

"Isn't that correct? Wasn't there a ninth woman?"

"I can't say whether there was or wasn't."

"And why can't you?"

"I can't say."

"You took eleven over there? To the house on the beach."

"Yes."

"We know where two went. We know where eight went. Do you know where the other woman is?"

Judge McKenzie leaned over the bench.

"Mr. Somerset, how did you know there were eight handled by the State Department? Let me see that document."

Somerset handed her the document.

"Your Honor, this memo that was furnished to us ... I'm not vouching for the accuracy of it. But that memo indicates the State Department resettled eight of these women."

Judge McKenzie scanned the document.

"This is a memo from someone in their legal department. Pat Frazer. A memo from Pat Frazer at the State Department to someone at Hogan Smith's office that says they were glad to have helped. 'I have been assured all eight are safely resettled. Will keep you advised.'"

Somerset nodded.

"I'm not vouching for Ms. Frazer's accuracy, Your Honor. I'm saying I have a document that suggests there were eight women. By Rev. Nolan's count there should have been nine. I want him to tell me where that ninth person is."

Judge McKenzie looked over at Scott.

"Rev. Nolan, do you know, for a fact, that there is one more person not accounted for by this memo and your testimony thus far?"

"I ... I cannot answer that question, Your Honor."

"Do you know where she is?"

"I cannot answer that question."

Judge McKenzie frowned.

"Are you claiming a privilege?"

"I cannot answer that question."

Judge McKenzie turned to Collins.

"Mr. Collins?"

Collins stood.

"Your Honor, my client cannot answer that question without putting this—"

Scott interrupted.

"Greg, you're fired."

Judge McKenzie swiveled her chair around to face Scott.

"Excuse me?"

"He's fired. Your Honor, Greg Collins no longer represents me.

He's fired."

"Rev. Nolan, you are very close to being in contempt of court. You know that, don't you?"

"I cannot answer the question. And neither will Mr. Collins. He is no longer authorized to speak on my behalf."

Judge McKenzie turned to Somerset.

"Mr. Somerset, where is the woman who married this Mr. Toombs?"

"She's here in Mobile County, Your Honor."

"Can't you get your information from her?"

"I have tried to, but she doesn't speak English very well and I don't understand whatever language it is she speaks, and I'm not sure she knows anything about what this witness might know. But I am trying to locate a translator who can help us. In the meantime I am entitled to answers from this witness, Your Honor."

Judge McKenzie turned back to Scott.

"Rev. Nolan, I know you just fired Mr. Collins, and that's your right, but I'm appointing him to represent you. Or, at least to consult with you." She glanced over at Collins. "Mr. Collins, you need to make sure he understands what could happen here today."

Collins stepped around the counsel's table.

"Yes, Your Honor."

Scott came down from the witness stand. Together they started down the aisle toward the door. Judge McKenzie spoke up.

"Not that way." She gestured over her shoulder. "Take him in back. There's a room next to my office. You can talk in there. I don't want him going outside the secure area here." She turned to the bailiff. "Jimmy, put somebody in the hall."

The bailiff rose from his desk and started across the room toward Scott. Judge McKenzie stood.

"We'll take a short recess."

Seventy-two

Tatiana walked up the sidewalk to the Birmingham Library and pushed open the door. The musty smell of books tickled her nose. She moved past the circulation desk and into the main hall. Before her, the room was filled with rows and rows of polished library tables, each one with a brass lamp and a green lampshade. She pulled a chair from one of the desks and sat down.

In a few minutes she heard a noise behind her. She turned around to see Gina Crosby. Tatiana smiled and stood.

Gina whispered.

"If you're ready, we can go now."

"I thought that man shot you."

Gina shook her head.

"He missed."

Gina took Tatiana by the arm.

"Come on. We need to get moving."

Gina glanced away. Tatiana followed her gaze. A man stood near the wall on the opposite side of the room. As they moved forward, he put his hand to his mouth. Tatiana could see his lips moving; then she noticed the wire that ran down his neck from his ear.

Outside, Gina and Tatiana walked to the street. A car waited there. As they came toward it, an agent stepped from the opposite side and opened the rear door. Gina pushed Tatiana inside. Someone closed the door behind them. The car started forward.

Seventy-three

An hour later the hearing in Judge McKenzie's courtroom resumed. Judge McKenzie turned to Collins.

"Mr. Collins, have you had an opportunity to explain things to Rev. Nolan?"

Collins stood.

"Yes, Your Honor."

"Rev. Nolan, come on up and take a seat at the witness stand. I remind you, you are still under oath."

Scott made his way to the witness stand.

"Rev. Nolan, have you consulted with Mr. Collins this morning on the matters we've been discussing?"

"Yes, Your Honor."

"And has he explained to you the consequences of being found in contempt of court?"

"Yes, Your Honor."

"And you are aware that refusing to obey an order of this court places you in contempt?"

"Yes, Your Honor."

"Rev. Nolan, having heard the testimony and argument presented here today, it is the order of this court that you answer Mr. Somerset's questions regarding this woman. Do you understand that?"

"I cannot answer his questions, Your Honor."

"Are you refusing to obey the order of this court?"

Scott did not reply. Judge McKenzie turned away.

"Very well. Rev. Nolan, I find you in contempt of court, and I order you confined to the county jail until such time as you choose to answer Mr. Somerset's questions." She glanced over at the bailiff.

"Jimmy. Take Rev. Nolan into custody."

The bailiff came from his desk and slipped a pair of handcuffs from his belt. Judge McKenzie stood.

"This hearing is adjourned."

Seventy-four

*T*atiana sat on the sofa and stared at the television. Across the room Gina sat on a chair near the door reading a magazine. Tatiana turned off the television and tossed the remote on the bed.

"I hate being like this."

Gina didn't bother to look up.

"You're safe."

Tatiana smiled.

"Yes. I am safe." She opened the minibar and took out a can of Coca-Cola. "Do you think they would have found me?"

"They were in Orlando two days after you left."

Tatiana's mouth fell open.

"In Orlando?"

Gina tossed the magazine aside.

"They found the woman at the Krystal."

"The woman with the phone?"

"Yes. And the other one. The one downtown."

Tatiana took a sip of Coke.

"Are they okay?"

"They're fine."

"How did they do that? How did they find them?"

"Traced the calls somehow."

A frown wrinkled Tatiana's brow.

"What happened? Did they do anything to them?"

"They're both fine. They didn't do anything to the lady from the Krystal."

"What about the other one?"

"They got a little rough with her."

"Rough with her? Why?"

"The first lady talked. The second told them to go away."

"Is she okay?"

Gina nodded.

"She's fine. She said if we saw you to tell you to shove it up their ..."

There was a knock at the door. Gina drew her pistol and pressed her face close to the peephole. She turned back to Tatiana.

"Did you order room service?"

Tatiana shook her head. Gina pointed to the bathroom.

"Get in there and don't come out."

Tatiana came around the bed. Gina pressed a button on her radio.

"Who's watching the hall?"

Seventy-five

$\mathcal{S}$cott was awakened by the clanging of metal as someone unlocked the cell door. He opened his eyes and glanced around, wondering what would happen next. The night before he'd seen two fights in the television room and heard another from the shower. He lay motionless on the cot and listened.

Footsteps moved toward him. A wooden baton tapped his feet.

"Let's go."

Scott rolled on his side and squinted against the light.

"What are we doing?"

"Garbage detail. They want you downstairs. Should have been there half an hour ago."

Scott swung his feet over the side of the cot.

"No one said anything to me about it."

The guard jabbed him in the side with the baton.

"Don't get smart with me. At least you get out of here for a while. Let's go."

Scott slipped on his shoes and stood. The guard pointed with the baton toward the hallway. Scott stumbled toward the cell door. The guard followed him out and guided him toward the elevator.

When the elevator doors opened downstairs, the guard led him past the booking section to the rear door. He pressed a button on the wall. A buzzer sounded. The door opened. The guard motioned with the baton. Scott walked through the doorway and found himself standing on a loading dock. A pickup truck was parked there, the engine idling. Three steel barrels sat in back.

The guard grumbled.

"Go with him."

Scott glanced down at the truck. A man in a tan uniform sat

behind the steering wheel. He wore a cap pulled low on his forehead and slumped against the door, arms folded across his chest, head bowed in a resting position. Scott made his way around to the passenger side and climbed inside. Before he could close the door, the driver sat up, put the truck in gear and started away from the building.

At the street the driver turned the truck to the right, pushed back the cap from his face, and smiled. Scott felt his heart jump. The man behind the steering wheel was David Brenner.

"What are you doing?"

The smile quickly vanished from Brenner's face.

"There's been some trouble."

Scott's eyes were wide.

"What kind of trouble?"

"They tried to get Tatiana."

"Where?"

"We picked her up at the library. Got her to a hotel. They came after her."

"How'd they know where she was?"

"We don't know yet."

The eastern sky was gray. In an hour the sun would be over the horizon. Scott looked over at Brenner.

"Where are we going?"

"We're moving her. We need you to help."

Seventy-six

*T*atiana stared at her reflection in the mirror and watched as tears rolled down her cheeks. In her hand she held a hairbrush, but her hand shook too much to lift it. All she could think about was how much someone wanted her to die.

An agent appeared in the doorway. She had been there most of the night, but Tatiana couldn't remember her name.

"Are you ready?"

Tatiana did her best to run the brush through her hair.

"Where is Gina?"

"She'll be along later."

"I thought she was coming with us."

"Don't worry about that. Just get ready. We need to get to the airport."

"We are flying?"

"Yes."

Tatiana shoved the brush in her overnight bag and wiped her eyes with a tissue, then turned from the mirror with a smile.

"Okay. I am ready."

Seventy-seven

*B*renner made a right onto Dauphin Street. Just past the Warren Building, he turned left into an alley and switched off the headlights. A car was parked there. Brenner brought the truck to a stop behind it.

"I think you know the man in that car." Brenner smiled over at Scott. "He knows what to do with you."

The only light in the alley came from the dim glow of a streetlight on the corner behind them. Even so, Scott recognized the distinctive shape of the car parked a few feet from the bumper of the truck. It was Mike Connolly's 1959 Chrysler Imperial. Scott had ridden in it many times.

From someplace deep inside, tears welled up in Scott's eyes. Brenner seemed not to notice.

"Go." He waved his hand in a shooing motion. "We've got a lot to do today."

Scott pushed the door open and jumped out. As he walked toward the car, he heard the engine start. Connolly grinned at him as he crawled onto the front seat.

"Father Scott." He stuck out his hand. Scott clasped it in his. Connolly cackled. "I've never helped a priest break out of jail before."

Scott laughed. The car started forward.

"Where are we going?"

"Home, man. Your house."

Scott raised his eyebrows in an approving look.

"A shower would be great."

They reached the end of the alley and turned onto Government Street. As they drove through midtown, Scott looked out the window.

He'd seen the city many times early in the morning when it was just coming to life, but somehow he'd missed the way the predawn light muted the stark white of the stately old houses and transformed the azaleas and oaks into garish, imposing figures.

"Jail is no place to be," he muttered.

He spoke without turning around. Behind him he felt Connolly's hand against the front seat.

"Now you see why I practice law."

Scott repeated himself in a whisper.

"It's no place to be."

Connolly spoke up.

"Listen, things have changed."

Scott turned to look at him, his thoughts suddenly jerked back to the present.

"What do you mean?" His eyes were wide. "Is Maggie all right?"

"Maggie's fine. She's waiting on you." Connolly hesitated a moment, then lowered his voice. "Hayford's dead."

Scott frowned.

"What happened to him?"

"Somebody shot him. They found him in his car. Parked over on Spring Hill Avenue. He was slumped over the steering wheel. He'd been shot in the back of the head."

Scott felt sick. He leaned his head back and rested it against the seat.

"Is that why they're moving Tatiana?"

"I don't know. She's coming here to testify before that federal grand jury. I don't know if Hayford's death had anything to do with the timing or not."

"Do they know who did it?"

"Oh, yeah. They know. I mean, they haven't said yet. But with the grand jury and this lawsuit, and you refusing to talk, they know why he was killed."

"That means there are only two people left who know what happened in that condo."

"I'd say it narrows things down."

Scott lowered the window. Damp morning air blew against his face. He closed his eyes and did his best to quiet his roiling stomach.

Seventy-eight

*F*BI agents guided Tatiana from her hotel room into the hall. Two more men were waiting there. Together they led her to a service elevator and rode downstairs to the kitchen. It was early in the morning, but already the kitchen was busy. No one seemed to notice as they made their way past the ovens and out the employee entrance.

A dark-blue sedan was parked in front of the loading dock. Tatiana hesitated. An agent took her by the arm and guided her toward it. When they reached the car, he opened the rear door and stood behind her as she ducked onto the seat. As she slid her legs out of the way, the agent slammed the door closed. Before she was settled, the car started forward.

At the street they turned right. In front of them a black Suburban moved away from the curb. Tatiana's heart skipped a beat, but no one in the car seemed concerned. She glanced out the rear window and saw a second Suburban following behind. She turned to face forward and watched out the window as they wound their way through the Birmingham streets.

Ten minutes later they came to the airport entrance. Tatiana leaned to one side and watched through the front windshield as they drove past the entrance, then continued around to the opposite side of the runway. A minute or two later they slowed and turned onto a parking lot behind a large hangar. The Suburban traveling in front of them parked behind the building. The car with Tatiana inside parked next to it. As they came to a stop, the glare of headlights washed over them.

Tatiana gasped. She turned to look out the rear window and saw the other Suburban had made a U-turn. It was now parked behind her at a right angle, shielding her car from view. The doors opened and four agents climbed out.

Someone opened the rear door of the car and motioned for her to get out. As she came from the car, she bumped against a man standing just inches away. He gave her a tight-lipped smile and scooted back to let her past. Behind him Tatiana saw three men waiting between the car and the Suburban. They hovered over her as she walked toward the hangar.

Inside, the men escorted her down a hallway to a door. On it in plain block letters were the words Authorized Personnel Only. One of the men reached around Tatiana and opened the door. Someone behind her held it open as she entered.

Beyond the door was a locker room. As Tatiana entered, Gina Crosby appeared from around the corner and grabbed the door handle. She nodded to the men.

"Thanks, guys. I have it."

The agents disappeared. Gina closed the door and smiled. Tatiana was relieved to see her. Gina gestured with her thumb over her shoulder.

"We're around here."

Tatiana followed her. Gina glanced back as they walked.

"Did you finally get to sleep?"

Tatiana nodded.

"A little."

Gina paused to let Tatiana draw even with her, then laid her hand gently against the small of Tatiana's back.

"That was a tense moment."

Tatiana managed to smile. She nodded nervously.

"I was scared."

Gina leaned closer and lowered her voice.

"So was I."

Tatiana nodded again. Tears came to her eyes. Gina looked away.

"We have some clothes for you to wear."

A few steps farther Tatiana passed a row of lockers and found two women standing there. Both of them were tall and slender with dark hair and round, dark eyes. Each of them had on a gray suit and a light-blue shirt. The women turned away.

Tatiana glanced at Gina.

"What are they—"

Gina pointed to a gray suit and a blue shirt hanging in an open locker.

"We wanted you to blend in with us, so we chose this outfit."

Tatiana nodded toward the other women.

"Who are they?"

Gina smiled.

"They are you."

Tatiana frowned.

"They are me?"

"Don't worry about it right now." Gina gestured toward the locker. "Just get these clothes on. In a few hours you'll be safe in Mobile." She pointed to a bench nearby. "Lay your old clothes here. We'll put them in with the rest of your stuff." Gina glanced at her watch. "Better get moving. We need to be ready."

Seventy-nine

Later that morning Scott stood in a hangar at the airport in Mobile and watched as a Gulfstream jet taxied past the commercial terminal. It slowed at the end of the runway and turned toward the hangar. Standing next to him was an FBI agent. As the plane made the turn, the agent nudged Scott with an elbow. Scott looked up. The agent handed him a small black object about the size of a pack of cigarettes. Made of black plastic, it had a button in the center and a small metal key ring at the top. Scott held it in the palm of his hand and remembered seeing a similar device that night in the room with Keyton Attaway when they were on the trip in the mountains. He looked up at the agent.

"What's this?"

The agent smiled.

"A panic button." He pointed to the button on the front. "If something happens, press that."

Scott gave him a blank look.

"If something happens?"

The agent nodded.

"Yeah." He pointed again. "If something happens, press that."

Scott swallowed.

"You mean, something could happen?"

The agent looked away.

"You never know."

Scott glanced down at the button once more.

"What happens when I press it?"

"The cavalry comes. Put it in your jacket pocket with the button facing out. That way, you can press it without having to get your hand inside your pocket."

Scott looked at it one last time, then slipped it inside his pocket. "What happens if I push it by accident?"

"Don't worry. No one will mind."

The sound of the jet engines grew louder as the plane approached. Scott's heart raced as the plane rolled through the doors and came to a stop inside. Two workmen chocked the wheels. Moments later the door swung open and the stairs unfolded. One of the workmen checked to make sure the stairs were properly in place, then disappeared behind the plane. Scott straightened his jacket and waited.

A woman appeared in the doorway. About six feet tall, she had short blonde hair. She wore a gray suit with a light-blue shirt and shoes with a low heel. From the doorway she glanced around, surveying the area, then started down the steps. Behind her was a tall, slender woman with dark hair. She was dressed in the same gray suit with a blue shirt. Scott smiled when he saw her.

The man standing beside Scott tapped him on the shoulder and started toward a car parked just off the tip of the airplane's wing. Scott followed him, but his eyes were on Tatiana. Something about her was different, the way she held her head, the way her hips moved when she walked. He couldn't quite put his finger on it, but something had changed.

As Tatiana reached the bottom of the steps, agents on the ground gathered around her, shielding her from view. They hustled her to the car, waited while she slipped inside, then closed the door. At the same time the door opened on the opposite side of the car and Scott slipped in beside her on the rear seat. He glanced over at her to say something, then stopped short.

Fear shot through him. The veins in his neck pulsed. His chest felt tight. The woman seated next to him wasn't Tatiana.

Scott turned away and stared out the window, trying to think of what to do. Then he remembered the panic button the agent had given him. He slid his hand over his jacket pocket and felt the device beneath his fingers. In his mind he recounted his conversation with the agent at his house that morning.

They were bringing Tatiana back. She was to appear before the grand jury. Powerful people already had tried to kill her. He should be there to meet her at the airport, let her see a familiar face right away so she wouldn't be afraid.

As Scott's mind recounted what the agent had said, his fingers curled around the door handle. Slowly, carefully, he pulled up on the handle and leaned against the door. Nothing happened. He tried again. Still it wouldn't move. He looked out the window, searching for the agent who'd been with him that morning. Before he could find him, the car started forward.

A black Suburban led the way as they drove from the hangar, across the tarmac, and around the building to a service road. Behind them a second Suburban followed.

Scott glanced at the agents seated up front. Neither of them had said a word since he got in the car. He studied them now from the backseat.

The driver was young. Not too young, but younger than the agents Scott had seen that morning. His hair was freshly cut, but the skin along his hairline was white. The skin of his neck and face was tanned. Scott stared at him for a moment, then looked across the seat to the passenger's side. The man seated there was heavier and older. There was a touch of gray in his hair, and Scott noticed a hole in his earlobe. The imprint of an earring was still visible in the flesh of the lobe.

The service road took them around the perimeter of the airport to a gate and the highway beyond. Guards at the gate held traffic at bay and let them pass unimpeded. They turned onto Airline Highway, picked up speed, and started toward town.

Slowly, Scott turned his head from the window and glanced across at the woman once more, just to make sure. This woman looked a lot like Tatiana. The resemblance was close, even uncanny. But it wasn't her. He'd seen Tatiana many times, and seeing this woman now, up close, he wondered how he'd ever thought it was her in the first place. As he looked at her, his fingertips traced the outline of the device in his pocket.

Through the windshield Scott saw an intersection up ahead. Schillinger Road, he thought. He glanced out the window beside him to make sure. Suddenly the car made a sharp turn to the right. Tires squealed as the car turned the corner.

Moments later the agent seated in front of Scott turned around to face the woman. As he did, his arm came over the seat. In his hand was an automatic pistol. Without a moment's hesitation, he pulled the trigger. A bullet struck the woman in the forehead. Her body went limp and slumped down the seat toward the floor. Blood spurted everywhere.

Scott's mouth dropped open. Before he could speak, the gunman pointed the pistol at him. For an instant Scott was sure he saw a smile on the man's face.

Suddenly the car swerved to the right, sending the gunman tumbling across the seat into the driver. The driver cursed, then swerved back to the left, sending the gunman sailing to the opposite side of the car.

Scott ducked low behind the front seat and pressed his fingers against the outside of his jacket pocket. Frantic, he jabbed at his pocket over and over, then shoved his hand inside and pressed the panic button again.

Car horns sounded. Tires screeched. The engine roared as the car picked up speed. By then the gunman had recovered. He swung his arm over the seat once more. Scott grabbed the barrel of the pistol. They struggled back and forth, Scott holding the barrel, the man twisting and tugging to jerk it free.

From out of nowhere a fist came over the seat and struck Scott on the jaw. Addled and confused, Scott refused to let go of the barrel. The gunman's fist rained down on him, striking blow after blow against Scott's head. Scott squeezed the barrel of the pistol tighter and grabbed the man's wrist with his free hand.

Just then something slammed into the car from the rear. The man with the pistol pulled free of Scott's grasp and fell forward against the dash. The pistol hit the windshield. Scott glanced out the back window and saw a black Suburban pushing them from behind. The driver of the car cursed. The engine raced even faster. The car pulled ahead.

In the front seat the gunman pulled himself to a sitting position and groped around the driver's feet for the pistol. Scott's fear turned to rage. He reached over the seat and grabbed for the steering wheel. The driver elbowed him in the face. The car swerved to the left and right. The driver threw another elbow. This one caught Scott between the eyes. He collapsed onto the rear seat.

While Scott clutched his nose, the driver reached beneath his jacket and drew a pistol. He held the steering wheel with his left hand and turned to look back at Scott. Peering between his fingers, Scott saw the end of the barrel pointed at his head. Unable to move, he waited for the fatal impact against his skull.

A shot rang out. Scott heard the bullet as it whizzed past his head. The driver glanced at the road, then back at Scott. As he lifted the pistol once more, Scott reached for it. At the last instant he shoved it to one side. As he did, the driver squeezed the trigger and blew out the rear window.

The gunman reached over the seat for Scott. Instead of a pistol he had the ends of a necktie wrapped around his hands like a gar-rote. His fingers grabbed Scott by the hair and pulled him close. Scott tried to get his arms up to protect his neck, but the gunman knocked them away. The silk tie felt smooth as it pulled tight against his neck.

Unwilling to give in, Scott pushed against the rear seat with his feet. His body slid over the front seat toward the man. Still the tie drew tighter. Scott kicked wildly and struggled for breath, gasping for air as he fought to remain conscious.

Suddenly a shot rang out. Warm, red blood splattered over Scott's face. The car horn sounded a long, continuous note. There was a rumbling sound and the car began to bounce. The tie around his neck slackened. Scott gasped for air. The car bounced more vio-lently. Scott felt himself slip free of the man's grasp. He pulled himself up with his legs and fell onto the rear seat.

The car bounced hard. Scott banged his head against the ceil-ing. His back slammed against the front seat. Then his feet came over his head as the car flipped over and came to rest on its top. Dust and dirt filled the air.

Beside him the woman's body lay lifeless and still. Blood from her forehead oozed onto Scott's leg. He pushed against her head to move it away, but it wouldn't budge. He tried again, then saw the driver's body wedged between the woman and the door. There was a gaping hole in the side of his head.

Scott turned away and vomited.

Eighty

*A*cross town the real Tatiana was aboard a Gulfstream jet on final approach to Brookley Field, a former Air Force base that was now an industrial park. When the plane landed, it taxied to a hangar on the back side of the complex. There she was escorted to a Suburban and whisked away. The streets were not barricaded. There was no motorcade, no sirens, no police escort. Just a simple, effective pickup and delivery. Twenty minutes after the plane landed, she was downtown in the secure parking deck beneath the federal courthouse. U.S. Marshals met her there and accompanied her upstairs to the grand jury room.

For the remainder of the day Tatiana sat before thirty-two grand jurors. For the first two hours she recounted events that had transpired at a condo in Orange Beach on an evening in the summer a year and a half ago. When she finished with that, they wanted to hear about Panama Tan and how she came to be in the United States. By the end of the day she was exhausted.

When the grand jury recessed that evening, FBI agents took Tatiana to the garage in the basement. From there they drove her back to Brookley Field. By sundown she was aboard a Gulfstream jet bound for a destination that only she and the pilot knew.

Eighty-one

*T*wo weeks later Scott sat in Mike Connolly's office, staring across the desk at the wall above Mike's head. Sunlight filtered through the blinds over the windows. Traffic noise drifted up from the street below. But in his mind all he could see was the man leaning over the seat of the car, the woman slumped beside him, the barrel of that pistol pointed at his head.

Connolly's chair creaked as he leaned it back.

"That drink cold enough?"

Scott nodded and took a sip of Boylan ginger ale, then set the bottle on the desk. He gave Connolly a thin, tight-lipped smile.

"You think they would have really left me in jail until I talked?"

Connolly shrugged.

"I don't know. Judge McKenzie's a good judge." He shrugged again. "There were some powerful people gunning for you." He folded his hands in his lap. "That took guts."

Scott rocked his chair on its back legs.

"What?"

"Saying no like that."

Scott shrugged.

"It didn't seem like much at the time." He dropped the chair forward. "You think Tatiana will be all right?"

Connolly scooted his chair up to the desk.

"I think she'll be fine."

Scott sighed and ducked his head.

"It seems like such a waste."

"A waste? What do you mean?"

"Hayford's dead. The lady riding in the car with me is dead. The driver's dead. And for what?" He looked up at Connolly. "It's been two weeks and that grand jury hasn't done a thing."

Connolly grinned.

"You haven't seen the paper."

Connolly bent over and disappeared behind the desk. When he raised up, he had a newspaper in his hand. He tossed the paper across the desk. Scott caught it upside down in his lap. He turned it over.

There in bold print was the headline: Hogan Smith Indicted.

Scott smiled.

"They got him."

Connolly nodded.

"You got him."

"I didn't do anything."

Connolly scoffed.

"Risked your life. Twice. Went to jail. Risked your reputation. Reached in your wallet to make it happen." Their eyes met. "That sounds like a lot to me."

Scott stared at the headline. He was glad Smith had been indicted, but all he could think of was the men in the car and the woman they had shot in the head. He looked up at Connolly.

"How do you suppose those two men got in that car? There must have been a dozen FBI agents in that hangar."

Connolly nodded.

"Someone in a powerful position made some calls, put someone in a squeeze, got them in there."

"Hogan Smith."

Connolly nodded.

"Hogan Smith." He picked up a paper clip from the desk and twirled it between his fingers. "Tatiana was the only one left who knew he was there that night. She saw the money. She heard what they were talking about."

"But who were they? The men he was meeting in the condo."

Connolly shrugged.

"I don't know. Guess we'll have to wait for the trial to find out. If we ever do."

Scott shook his head. He leaned back in the chair and closed his eyes.

For the first time in weeks his mind wandered past the car and the pistol pointed at his head. He thought of the night he'd gone to the tanning salon to find Raisa. A fishing trip with Keyton Attaway and John Agostino. The smile on Keyton's face the last time he saw him.

After a moment he heard a chair move. He opened his eyes to see Connolly standing next to him, holding his jacket. Scott frowned at him.

"What's that for?"

"It's your jacket."

"I can see that. You throwing me out?"

"Taking you to work."

Scott closed his eyes again.

"I'm not ready to go to work."

Connolly took him by the arm.

"I remember a time when all I wanted to do was sit in that church of yours and stare at the windows. You told me I couldn't sit there. I had to get up and get in the fight."

Connolly tugged at his arm. Reluctantly, Scott stood. Connolly slipped the jacket sleeve over Scott's hand and pulled it up to his shoulder.

"Now that's what I'm telling you." He looked Scott in the eye. "Recess is over. Time to get back to work."

Scott slipped the jacket into place and gently straightened the sleeves. A lump formed in his throat. He looked over at Connolly.

"I've never been so afraid in my life."

Tears filled Connolly's eyes.

"I know."

Author Interview

1. How did you start writing? What was your first piece of writing?

I can't remember my first written piece, but I remember the first time I thought someone might like to read something I'd written. It was an eleventh-grade term paper about Walt Whitman. The teacher liked it, and I acquired my favorite quote: "Do I contradict myself? Very well, then, I contradict myself. I am large—I contain multitudes" (Walt Whitman, *Leaves of Grass*).

2. Why do you write fiction?

Stories are the way I understand life. I often forget people's names. I almost never forget their stories. It's how I make sense of things. It's how I think. How I view the events of my own life. When I write, I'm not a writer at a desk; I'm a construction foreman on a large project, clearing the site, digging the foundation, building the walls. Or I'm an artist painting a picture, brush stroke after brush stroke, laying on color after color until it looks just right. Or a singer, laying down track after track in the studio, searching for exactly the right sound. When I'm on the road signing books, I'm not a writer who wishes he was back at home writing. I'm Elvis before he was Elvis. On the road. Every night, another town. Life is a story. It's who I am.

3. What is the power of story?

Imagination. A reader doesn't read a story as an objective observer. He or she becomes the story. A participant. And as a participant, the reader engages the story with emotion. The story isn't words on a page; it's an experience, one that finds a place in the reader's memory. A memory that creates conflict in the reader's mind and lingers as that conflict is resolved. That's the power of story—the power to move a reader.

4. What do you hope readers will take away from your books?

Every story has a point. *The Sun Also Rises* (Hemingway), *The Celebrated Jumping Frog of Calaveras County* (Twain), or *The Firm* (Grisham)—they all have a point, a message, a subject or issue about which the writer was thinking and about which the writer wants the reader to think. I hope readers have an experience with my books that makes them think. I hope my books take them on a journey, and I hope they find the point I had in mind, but they'll have to find it on their own. I'm not telling.

5. Which character in this book is most like you?

Every character in every book comes from somewhere inside the writer. Fiction—readable, entertaining fiction—cannot be written any other way. Every character in my books is some part of me. In these Mike Connolly mysteries I suppose I identify most with Mike Connolly, but that primarily is because he is the character most fully developed. I had to go deeper into myself to find more of him, and in doing that, he became more of me.

6. What actor would you picture playing Mike Connolly in a movie?

Robert Duvall can play any character in any story I've ever written. Give me a call, Bobby, and bring Tommy Lee Jones with you.

7. Which writers have influenced you most?

Mark Twain and Ernest Hemingway—in that order. I first encountered Mark Twain at the age of seven. What a storyteller. But it was Hemingway who most influenced my writing style. Sparse, lean prose. Develop the characters through realistic dialogue. Don't answer every question about the characters. Don't fill in every detail about the story. There's nothing like a Hemingway novel.

8. Describe your writing process.

As a former attorney, I believe that all good writing begins with a legal pad and a black pen. I write out the story idea in one or two sentences. Next, I find a character through whom I can tell that story. I then write out the ending of the book. That's how I prepared for jury trials, and it's a good way to lay out a story. With those things in place, I figure out the chapters with a single sentence for each chapter. Finally, I turn on the computer and start writing out what I see in my mind.

9. Can you share a particularly memorable encounter with a reader?

I remember a lady who came to a book signing in Shreveport, Louisiana. Her name was Connie. She'd come there with a group from Monroe to attend a concert. They arrived early and wandered into the store while they waited. She bought one of my books. It was the first time she'd ever purchased a book signed by the author. I still remember the look on her face.

10. What is one fact about yourself that readers might find most surprising?

I once "mooned" the president of the United States. Actually it was unintentional. I was changing clothes in the parking lot at the

Pentagon when his helicopter flew over. He flew right over my car at the most inopportune moment. There was nothing to do but wave.

OTHER BOOKS BY JOE HILLEY

SOBER JUSTICE
DOUBLE TAKE
ELECTRIC BEACH
NIGHT RAIN

To learn more about Joe and his books,
visit his Web site at www.joehilley.com.

Invite Joe Hilley to Your Book Club

Transport your book club behind the scenes and into a new world by inviting Joe Hilley to join in your group discussion via phone. To learn more, go to www.cookministries.com/readthis or e-mail Joe directly at mikeconnollymysteries@yahoo.com.